P9-CAJ-286

POKÉMON™
SUPER
ACTIVITY BOOK:
DO YOU KNOW UNOVA?

PIKACHU PRESS™

$12.99 USA
$14.99 CAN

The Pokémon Company
INTERNATIONAL

Publisher: Heather Dalgleish
Publishing Manager: Amy Levenson
Writer: Lawrence Neves
Designer: Chris Franc
Art Director: Eric Medalle
Product Approval Manager: Phaedra Long
Product Approval Associate: Katherine Fang
Editor-in-Chief: Michael G. Ryan
Editors: Eoin Sanders, Hollie Beg and Wolfgang Baur
Acknowledgements: Kellyn Ballard and Blaise Selby

Published in the United States by
The Pokémon Company International
333 108th Avenue NE, Suite 1900
Bellevue, WA 98004
Visit us on the Web at www.pokemon.com

Printed in Shenzhen, China.

The Pokémon Company
INTERNATIONAL

This book was produced by Walter Foster Publishing, Inc. Walter Foster is a registered trademark.

ISBN: 978-1-60438-156-6

POKÉMON™
SUPER
ACTIVITY BOOK:
DO YOU KNOW UNOVA?

TABLE OF CONTENTS

INTRODUCTION

Hello, Pokémon adventurers! Welcome to the *Pokémon Super Activity Book: Do You Know Unova?* As you train for your journey to be the best Pokémon Trainer ever, you'll need to keep a sharp mind and a keen eye—and we're going to help you! Check out this gigantic book of mind-twisting puzzles and fun, interactive games we've assembled! Play by yourself or with a friend as you try to uncover the secrets of the Pokémon of the Unova region!

FIRE TYPES

WORD SEARCH—FIRE!

Hey, Trainers! Finding Pokémon is sometimes a tricky thing. You need patience, practice, and a keen eye. Try to find elusive Fire-type Pokémon in this word search—but beware, there are other Pokémon lurking here! We just want the Fire types (that includes dual types like Pignite, which is both a Fire and Fighting type)!

C X J S G L E Q E E O L N N B H B W L V R G K L V
H Z B U I T P A F P T R F L I T W I C K S W E T O
A B M V W M E B I X J L E M X S C P C J I X G V L
N K B S F G I K B E G J P A N S E A R Z J T Y U C
D R T A T N E S O C Z H I B H J Y F D E N T G I A
E W W R W H N Y E O Y H G H Y D N E R E M P K N R
L F L F K U E V O A A D N O D A M M P X L B K Z O
U R J J H B S A Y H R G I V H Q Q M O V O F O E N
R Q N T D E K V M X L B T A H T A S E E I R R A A
E R J Z E A A V F W M M E C M L A R V E S T A H R
K V I H M P H T Z N M Z B L P F C A M W Y Y U B G
S B I U U L I C M O B O W V V W H S C Q A S L I I
R J R Z P X H G A O M K D K S F M X M D A Y O G C
H A D O M I F G X H R Q V A J M Y K Y R H D Z O K
D A R M A N I T A N R H F Z L N X D R Y F C D P R

Tepig

Darmanitan

Simisear

Chandelure

Volcarona

Larvesta

Darumaka

Pignite

Litwick

Heatmor

Emboar

Pansear

Lampent

Turn to page 181 for the answers.

POKÉMON FINDER

Okay, so you know how to recognize a Pokémon by name!
Now let's see if you can catch Pokémon by instinct alone!

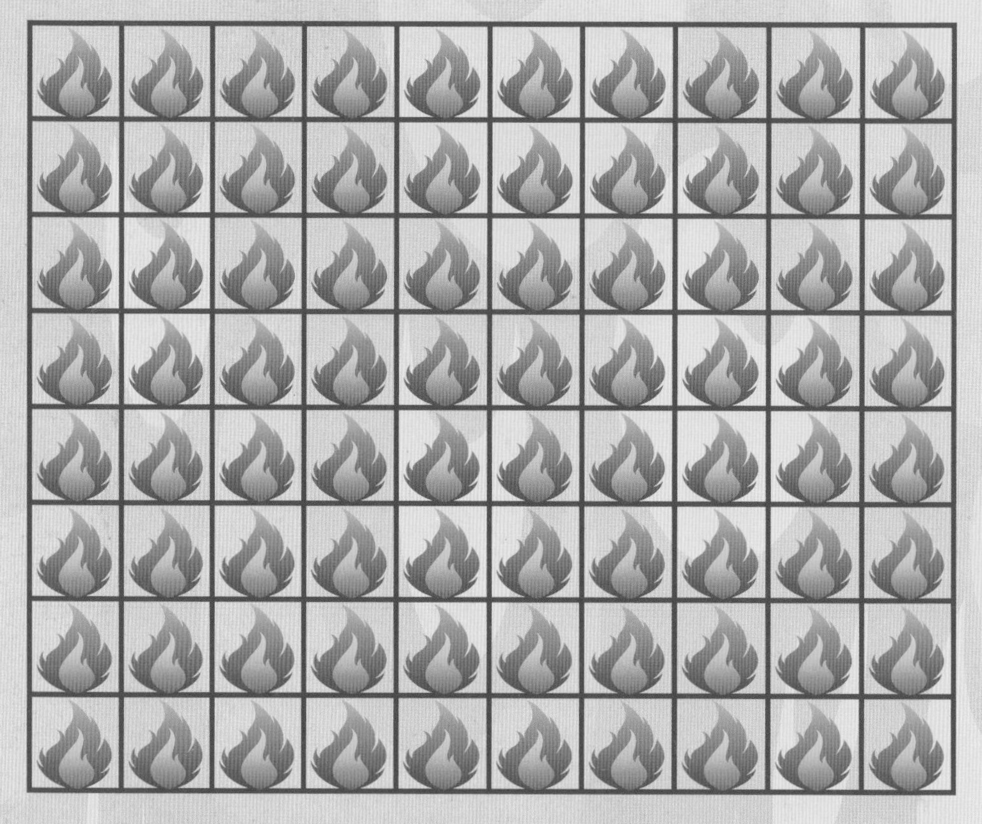

RULES: Hidden in this grid of fire are ten Pokémon! Take a pen, pencil, or crayon and mark off where you think the ten Pokémon are hiding. Check your score below to see how you did!

LEGEND

0–3 catches: You'll be awesome on our Pokémon team!
4–7 catches: You're doing really well! You'll be a Trainer in no time!
7–10 catches: Wow! Maybe you should head up a team of your own!

Turn to page 181 for the answers.

FIND THE DIFFERENCE

Okay, adventurer. You're getting better! Now see if you can spot the difference between these Pokémon! Being a good Trainer means that you can tell an impostor Pokémon from a real one—test your skill at spotting which Pokémon isn't quite right! Check colors, body parts, expressions—anything that can make a difference! Good luck!

Turn to page 181 for the answer.

MATCH THE MOVE

Now that you can spot the Pokémon with ease, let's find out if your knowledge goes beyond simply recognizing them! On the left are three Pokémon. On the right are the moves that go with each of those Pokémon. Match the Pokémon with the move that it can learn—let's see what you're made of!

Turn to page 181 for the answers.

POKÉMON SEEK AND FIND

So, you know your Pokémon?

Okay, let's see if you can spot the Pokémon in the following group by type!

Find two Fire types in this collage of Unova Pokémon!

Turn to page 181 for the answers.

FIGHTING TYPES

EVOLUTION REVOLUTION

Okay, Trainer! You are definitely on the path to greatness! Now, see if you know what your Pokémon will look like after they've evolved! Guess which Pokémon is missing from the Evolution cycle on this page. If you guess correctly, you really know how to brawl with the best of the Fighting-type Pokémon!

Turn to page 181 for the answer.

A PUZZLE OF POKÉMON

Let's see how well you can assemble the information at hand to help identify Pokémon—draw a line from each puzzle piece to where it should go in the puzzle!

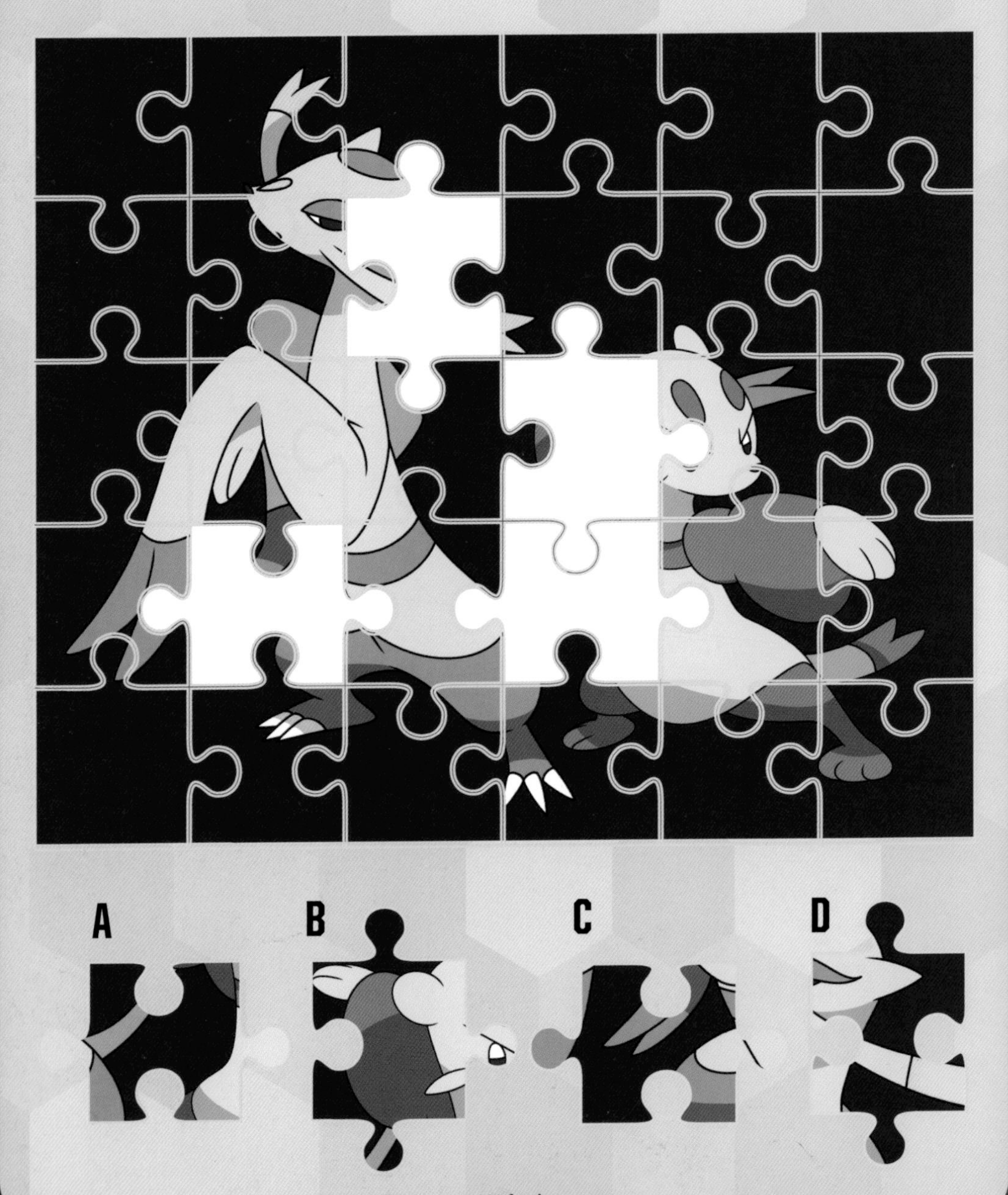

Turn to page 181 for the answers.

ODD POKÉMON OUT!

So you know your Pokémon by sight, but can you show your expertise and sort out the Pokémon that stand out in a crowd?

RULES: For this test, we're going to show you some different Pokémon. One of these Pokémon doesn't belong in the group, but which one? And what is the group? We'll give you three clues. You score yourself by how many clues you used!

CLUE #1: Some of these Pokémon have gotten quite far.

CLUE #2: There has been a change.

CLUE #3: My, how they've evolved.

SCORE

1 clue: Wow! Maybe you should head up a team of your own!

2 clues: You're doing really well! You'll be a Trainer in no time!

3 clues: You'll be awesome on our Pokémon team!

Turn to page 181 for the answer.

POKÉMON SUDOKU

Trainers should keep themselves sharp, both in mind and body—and Sudoku is a great way to keep your wits sharp! Use just the numbers 1–9. Each number can appear only one time in a row, column, and box. Go to it, Trainers!

4	7			5	9	8	3	
2	5	1	6		8		7	9
8		3	7		1	5	2	
	6	4	9	2	3	7		8
9	3		1	8		6	5	4
7	1		4		5		9	3
6	4			9	2	1	8	7
		9	8	7			6	
3	8	7	5	1		9	4	2

Turn to page 181 for the answers.

TYPE CAST!

Pokémon identification requires that a Trainer also know the type of Pokémon he or she is facing. This is extremely important when battling Pokémon, since type advantages can easily turn a battle! So, see if you can match the Pokémon on the left with their types on the right.

FIRE-FIGHTING

FIGHTING

DARK-FIGHTING

Turn to page 181 for the answers.

PSYCHIC TYPES

IT'S ALL IN YOUR MIND!

How well do you know Psychic types, Trainer? Let's see if you can answer a few questions about their habits, Evolutions, and moves. If you can figure this out, you deserve a gold star!

1 2 3 4 5 6 7 8 9 10 11 12 13 14

ACROSS

6. What is the first Psychic-type Pokémon that Ash encounters in Unova?

8. What Dragon-type Pokémon travels alongside Iris?

10. Which team has a Woobat?

12. What is the name of the scientist who rescued Musharna?

13. What powerful Psychic-type Pokémon does not evolve?

DOWN

1. What is the area where scientists originally did research on Pokémon dreams?

2. What is the last Evolution of Gothita?

3. Which of the following is both Psychic and another type? Gothorita, Duosion, or Swoobat?

4. Name one of the two types that Psychic types are most effective against.

5. What is the middle stage in this Evolution chain: Solosis, __________, Reuniclus?

7. What is the substance that Munna and Musharna use to reveal dreams?

9. What Pokémon evolves into Musharna?

11. What does Beheeyem evolve from?

14. Name one of the three types that are most effective against Psychic types.

Turn to page 181 for the answers.

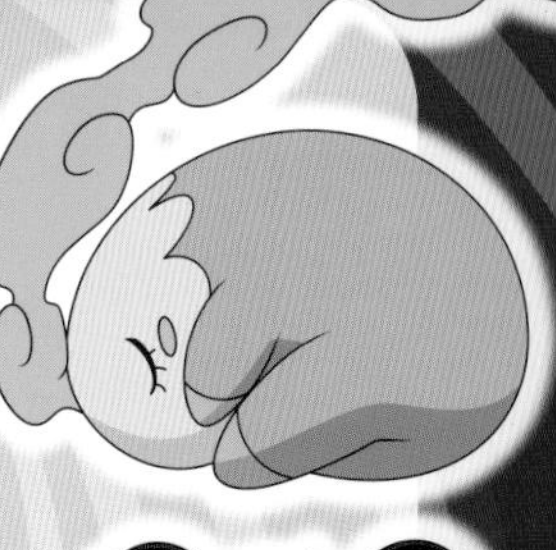

HAIKU

Pokémon Trainers know there is a special relationship between a Pokémon and its Trainer. Love, friendship, and happiness will make any Pokémon grow! And now you can pen a piece of poetic prose for your Psychic-type Pokémon! Fill in the blanks, and be as creative as you can be!

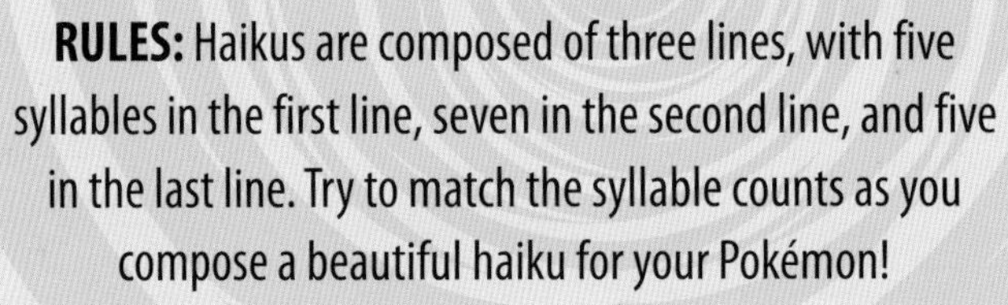

RULES: Haikus are composed of three lines, with five syllables in the first line, seven in the second line, and five in the last line. Try to match the syllable counts as you compose a beautiful haiku for your Pokémon!

HAIKU

To ______________________________
(Psychic-type Pokémon)

I knew we were ____________________.
(one, friends, good)

You ________________ **my** ______________
(know, sense, feel) (thoughts, smile, joy)

and are _________________.
(calm, glad, cool)

Yet I ______________ ________________.
(never, always) (grinned, stayed, smiled)

WALL SCRAWL

Your adventure has led you to some clues about Pokémon in your area! Other explorers seem to have left messages about the Pokémon they've seen. Can you decipher these hastily worded scrawls?

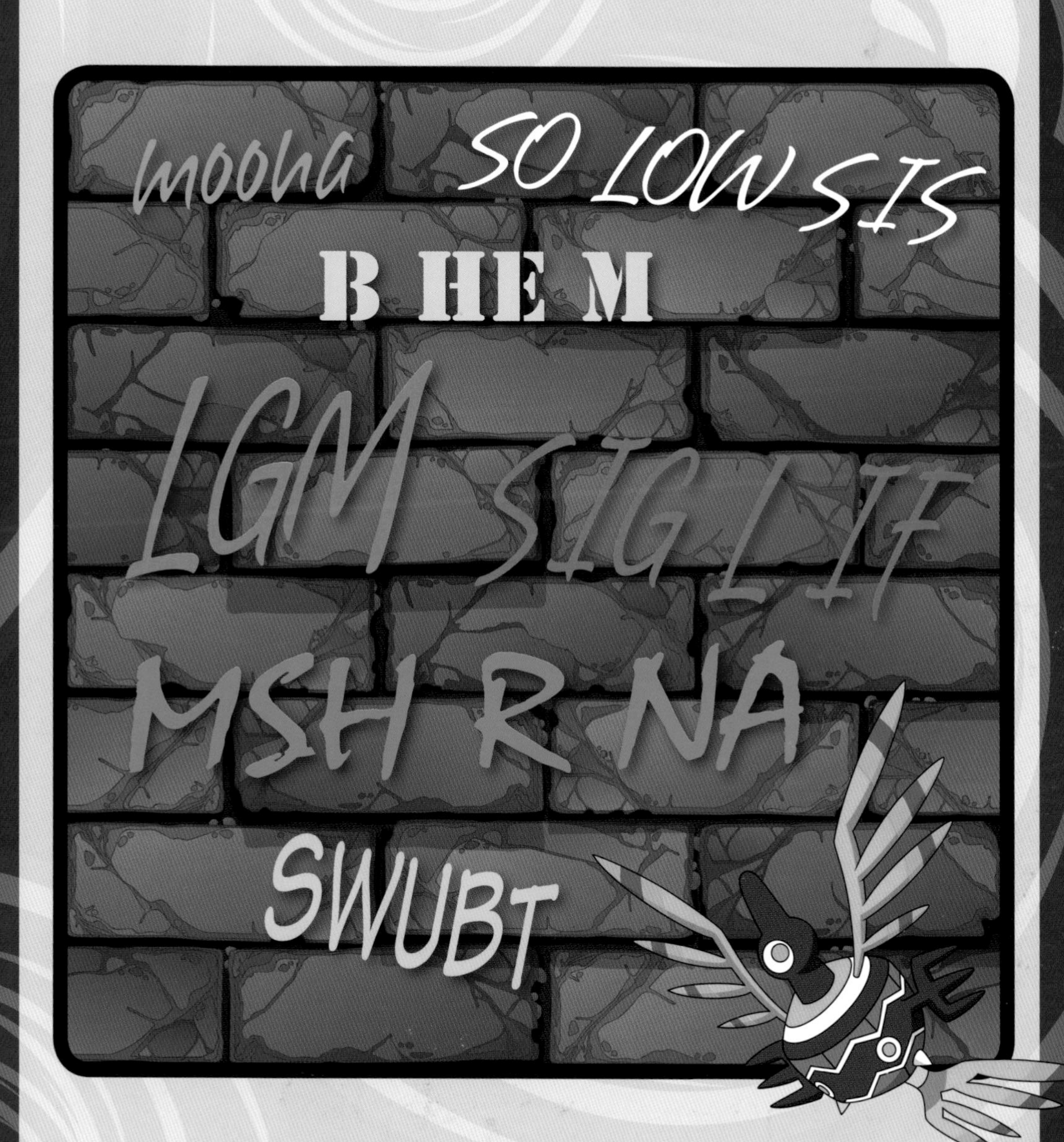

Turn to page 181 for the answers.

HELP MUNNA!

Munna and Musharna were working with Dr. Fennel when suddenly they got separated! Help Munna find its friend in this maze. Watch out, though—the maze gets kind of crazy!

END

START

Turn to page 181 for the answer.

FINISH THIS POKÉMON!

Can you remember what the different colors of a Pokémon look like? You're a Trainer, so you should be able to correctly color this Pokémon using only your memory. You should have no trouble at all, right? Good luck! See if you know your Pokémon as well as you think you do!

Turn to page 181 for the answer.

TRAINER PAGES

ASH

WHO'S YOUR FRIEND?

Knowing other Trainers in the Unova region is helpful, and you may even form bonds with others that will last a lifetime! Check your knowledge of other Trainers in Unova by correctly guessing which Pokémon travel with this Trainer!

Ash is the original, the one and only, a boy whose goal in life is to become a Pokémon Master! In the Unova region, he has met Pokémon he's never seen before. Which of these Pokémon has Ash already caught?

ASH KETCHUM

Turn to page 182 for the answers.

TRAVEL CHECKLIST

Are you ready to go out in the world and make your mark as a Trainer? Make sure you have a travel checklist handy. Which of the following items would you decide not to take with you?

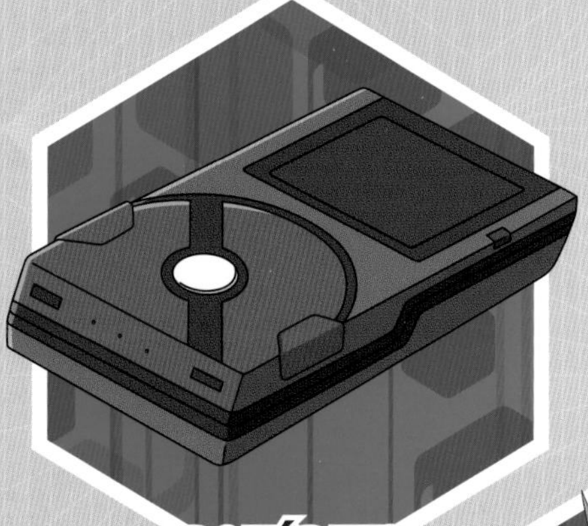

POKÉDEX?

PAPERWORK?

BERRIES?

A PICTURE FRAME?

XTRANSCEIVER?

Turn to page 182 for the answers.

DOTS WHAT I'M TALKING ABOUT!

Stay focused, Pokémon adventurer! Sometimes it may seem like your senses are playing tricks on you! Don't worry—a good Trainer knows that sometimes things are not what they seem. Look closely at this picture. See if you can spot the hidden Pokémon—we'll even give you a few clues!

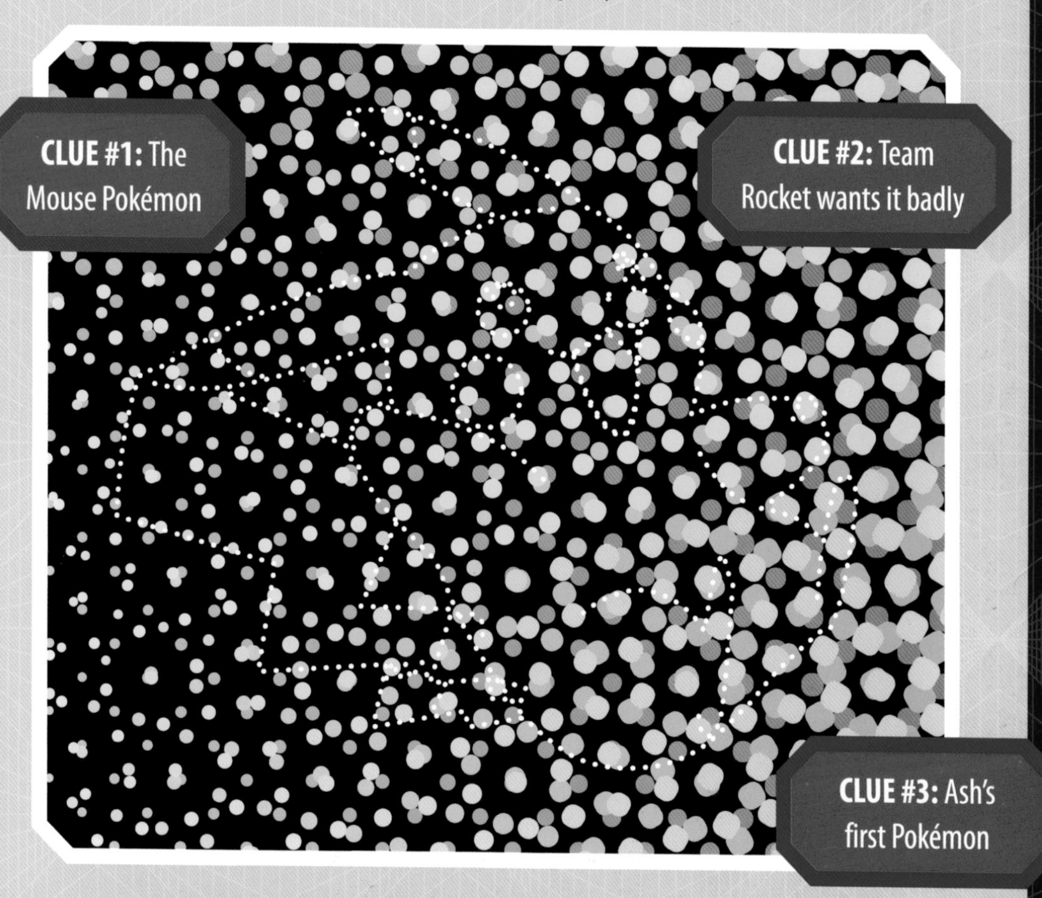

SCORE

1 clue: Wow! Maybe you should head up a team of your own!

2 clues: You're doing really well! You'll be a Trainer in no time!

3 clues: You'll be awesome on our Pokémon team!

Turn to page 182 for the answer.

LOOK! QUICK!

Wow! As far as Trainers go, you're shaping up to be one of the best! Now, speaking of shapes, let's see if your visual skills are still sharp.

When traveling throughout Unova, a Trainer will encounter different shapes in the tall grass, abandoned structures, and deep caves. Are those shapes just playing tricks on your eyes, or are they actually Pokémon? See if you can match these silhouettes to the Pokémon they belong to! Draw a line from the outline to the Pokémon it looks like. Good luck!

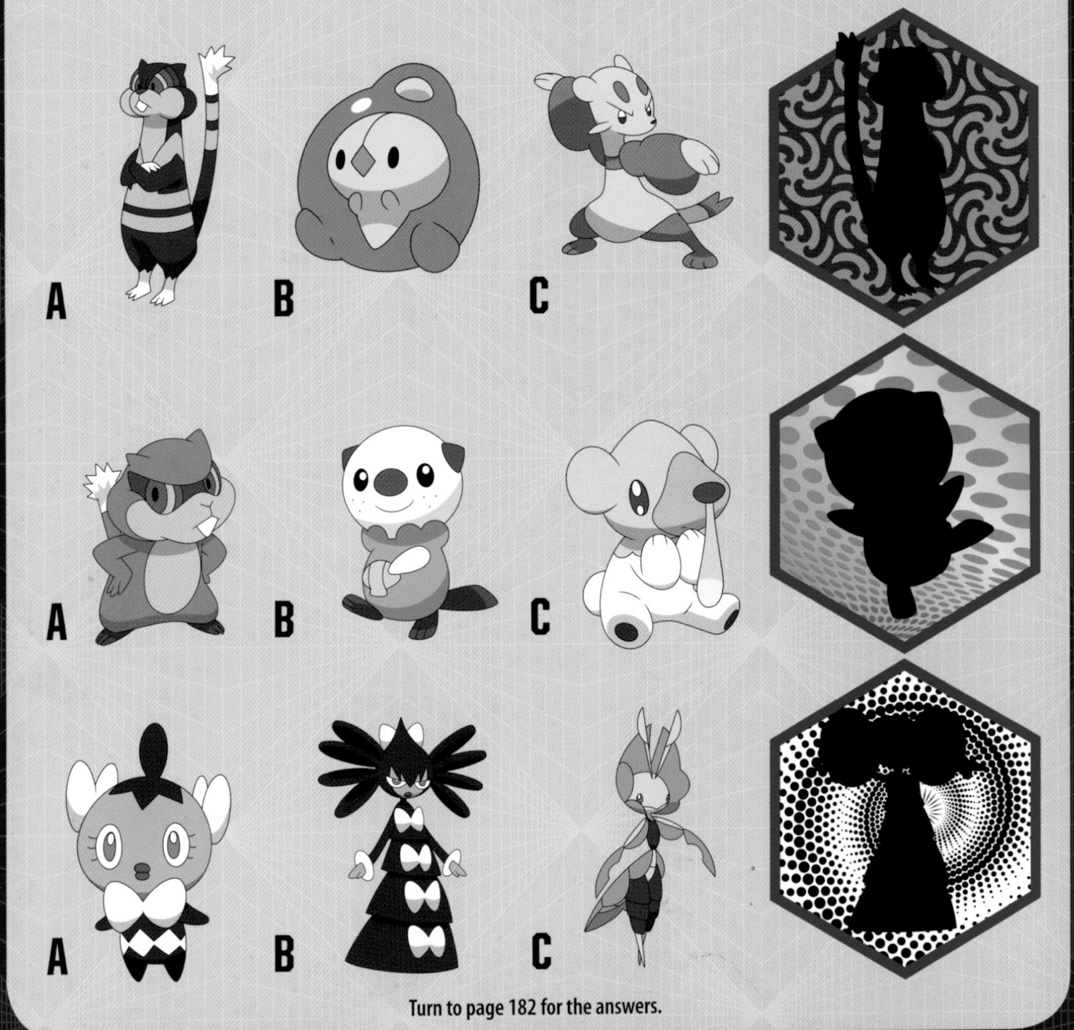

Turn to page 182 for the answers.

THE POKÉMON NAME GAME

Speed means a lot to a Trainer! Identifying your Pokémon and knowing their capabilities immediately is a key component of your training. Here's a one-, two-, or multi-player word game that tests how quick you are with your Pokémon.

RULES: You and a friend pick out a Unova Pokémon. Each of you then writes that Pokémon's name down on a piece of paper. Now, come up with as many words as you can from the letters in that Pokémon's name, within a two-minute time limit! The player with the most words wins!

EXAMPLE:

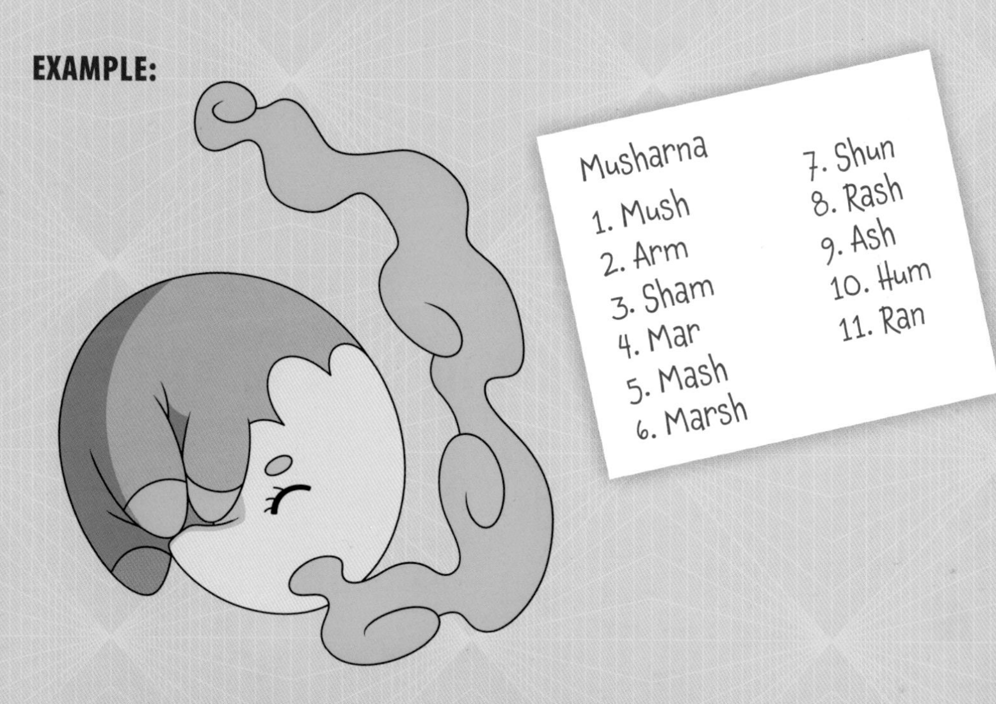

BONUS

Use the memory cards in the back of this book. Flip them face down, then pick one card and use the Pokémon on that card as your choice. If you pick a Psychic-type Pokémon, you score a five-point bonus!

CRYPTOGLYPHICS

Can you decipher the following coded message?
Use the clues from the Pokémon that we've found so far. . .

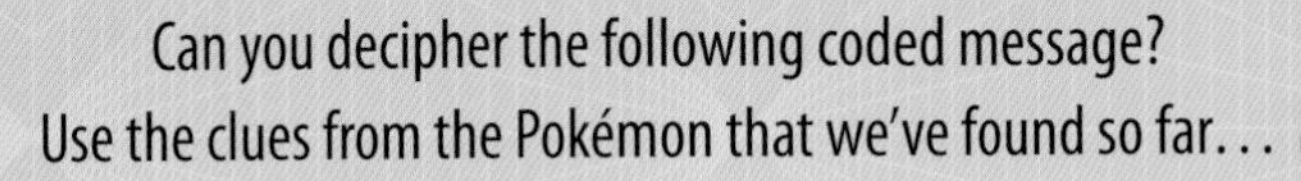

_ _ _ _ _ _ _ is unable to use

its _ _ _ _ _ _ _ _-type moves

because of a mysterious

_ _ _ _ _ _ _ _ _ _ _ _!

Does this have anything to do

with the Legendary Pokémon

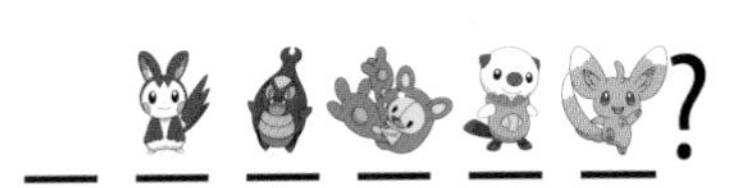

_ _ _ _ _ _?

LEGEND

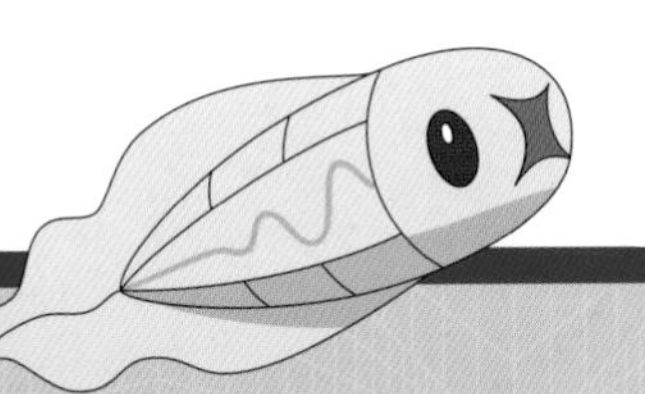

Turn to page 182 for the answers.

KNOWLEDGE BASE

Here are some slightly more difficult questions that only a seasoned Trainer would be able to answer. Get these all right and you're definitely a real Pokémon fan!

1. What is the first town Ash finds himself in when traveling to Unova?

   ____

2. Which Pokémon is traveling with Ash?

   ____

3. What's the name of the professor in the Unova region?

   ____

4. What three Pokémon does the professor show to Ash?

   ____

5. What Pokémon does Trip choose?

   ____

6. What Trainer ends up with an Emolga?

   ____

7. When Pikachu's Electric-type moves are disabled, what move does it whip out when facing Trip's Snivy for the first time?

   ____

8. Which Pokémon hatched from its Egg—and immediately attacked Pikachu?

   ____

9. In the Pinwheel Forest, Pikachu is attacked by the Sewing Pokémon, also known as ______________________________?

10. What move does a Ducklett use that turns Oshawott's face bright red?

    ____

Turn to page 182 for the answers.

WORD SCRAMBLE

A lot of training can be puzzling. You have to decipher a Pokémon's moods, its intentions, and even, at times, its behavior. A lot of the work involved in training your Pokémon is reading between the lines and sensing what your Pokémon wants or needs before it has to tell you.

RULES: Unscramble each word. In the letters that form that word, there is a secret letter that is surrounded by a box. Those letters will spell out the answer!

QUESTION

What is one secret to winning your battles in Unova?

1. Before evolving into Zebstrika, what was this Pokémon named?

LEBTZIL _ _ _ ☐ _ _ _

2. What is the first Evolution of Tynamo called?

KITEEKREL _ _ _ _ _ _ ☐ _ _

3. This Pokémon is Rufflet's Evolution.

VBARIYAR _ _ ☐ _ _ _ _ _

4. This Pokémon is Ash's companion.

KICPUAH _ ☐ _ _ _ _ _

5. This Pokémon feels flat, but it's "stunning".

NKSTSUIF _ _ _ ☐ _ _ _ _

6. Galvantula evolves from which Pokémon?

KOILTJ _ _ _ _ ☐ _

7. This Legendary Pokémon rules with the power of lightning.

DURSUHUNT _ _ _ ☐ _ _ _ _ _

8. Cilan used this Pokémon in his Gym in Striaton City.

AGESPNA _ _ _ _ _ ☐ _

ANSWER

☐ ☐ ☐ ☐ ☐ ☐ ☐ ☐

Turn to page 182 for the answers.

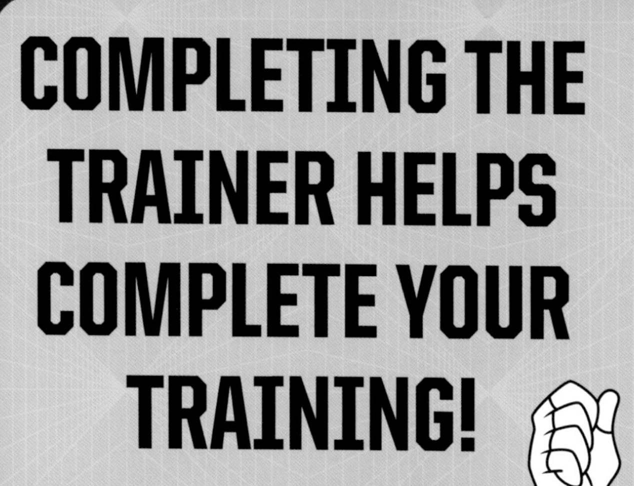

COMPLETING THE TRAINER HELPS COMPLETE YOUR TRAINING!

Okay, okay, we'll give you this—you know your Pokémon! Now, get to know the most famous Trainer around! We're sure you know him—he's a Trainer whose best friend also happens to be a Pokémon! Finish the picture and color in the rest of Ash!

Turn to page 182 for the answer.

POKÉMON ACROSTICS!

Let's play a game to help you get to know your Pokémon. This is a fun game that can be played with one, two, or multiple players.

RULES: Pick a Pokémon name. Write that name in a column. If you picked Pikachu, you should have a puzzle that looks like this:

Now, try to spell the longest word you can with the letters in each row. For example, starting with the first row, try to spell a word that starts with P, but is very long—like personality! You can only make one word per row, but you get one point for each letter used. Try for the longest word you know!

BONUS

Time the game—see how many words you can come up with in two minutes!

BONUS

Use the memory cards in the back of this book. Flip them face down, then pick one card and use the Pokémon on that card as your choice. If you pick an Electric-type Pokémon, you score a five-point bonus!

Pokémon Super Activity Book:
Do You Know Unova?
Certificate of
Completion
This is to show that
____
is a
Fire-type
Pokémon Specialist
Fighting-type
Pokémon Specialist
Psychic-type
Pokémon Specialist
Issued this ______ day of
____________________, 20_____.

GRASS TYPES

WORD SEARCH—GRASS!

So finding Fighting-type, Fire-type, and Psychic-type Pokémon proved to be pretty easy, huh? Well, let's take a look at what Grass-type Pokémon have in store for you! Once again, beware of other Pokémon that are not Grass types lurking here! You only want to find the Grass types or dual types like Sewaddle (which is a Bug- and Grass-type Pokémon)!

R	U	D	O	S	E	W	A	D	D	L	E	N	Q	S	I	M	I	S	A	G	E	K	L	I	N	K	W
D	D	W	S	G	L	N	K	O	E	V	O	W	F	C	E	E	S	C	A	V	A	L	I	E	R	W	T
S	P	F	I	W	B	B	Y	V	I	R	I	Z	I	O	N	B	O	N	M	G	X	G	O	L	E	T	T
P	W	E	F	V	A	C	O	T	T	O	N	E	E	K	F	E	R	R	O	S	E	E	D	Y	D	S	V
T	E	R	S	P	A	D	D	S	A	W	S	B	U	C	K	O	M	A	O	B	I	E	Y	Y	U	H	E
B	Y	C	P	E	T	I	L	I	L	Z	T	X	X	Y	H	N	D	X	N	J	H	D	O	T	G	O	X
T	W	H	I	M	S	I	C	O	T	T	X	P	G	T	D	E	L	B	G	T	S	W	C	F	Z	P	L
R	P	X	J	B	E	V	D	V	O	D	F	V	O	P	P	S	I	K	U	Z	E	A	L	P	Q	U	E
B	O	L	D	O	R	E	E	X	Y	N	W	R	X	I	O	O	L	K	S	V	R	I	S	W	A	S	A
B	P	Y	J	H	I	O	E	I	H	A	R	G	N	M	Z	D	L	F	S	A	P	K	N	C	A	E	V
D	R	I	L	L	B	U	R	R	A	E	D	E	B	A	D	W	I	Q	M	S	E	Y	I	O	F	R	A
M	N	N	Q	G	J	S	L	P	F	S	V	Y	L	T	C	A	G	K	D	I	R	D	V	C	T	V	N
P	A	N	S	A	G	E	I	T	C	W	D	F	X	Z	U	F	A	G	Q	I	I	M	Y	B	Q	I	N
H	I	X	X	H	P	Z	N	R	U	F	F	L	E	T	P	L	N	R	J	F	O	K	U	Q	J	N	Y
C	W	E	F	O	O	N	G	U	S	M	S	E	Q	Z	W	X	T	X	L	O	R	U	B	X	Q	E	P

Turn to page 182 for the answers.

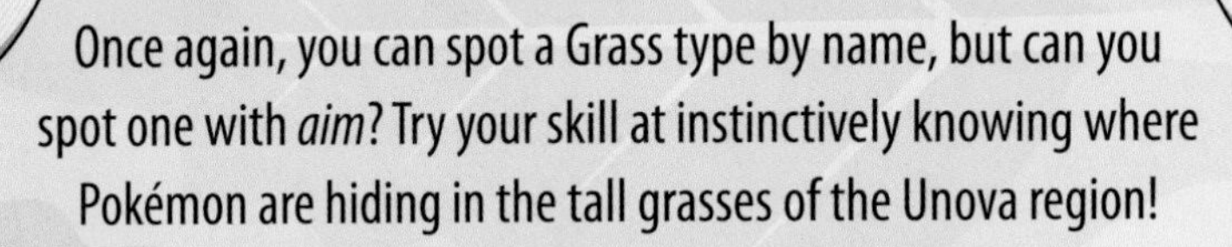

POKÉMON FINDER

Once again, you can spot a Grass type by name, but can you spot one with *aim*? Try your skill at instinctively knowing where Pokémon are hiding in the tall grasses of the Unova region!

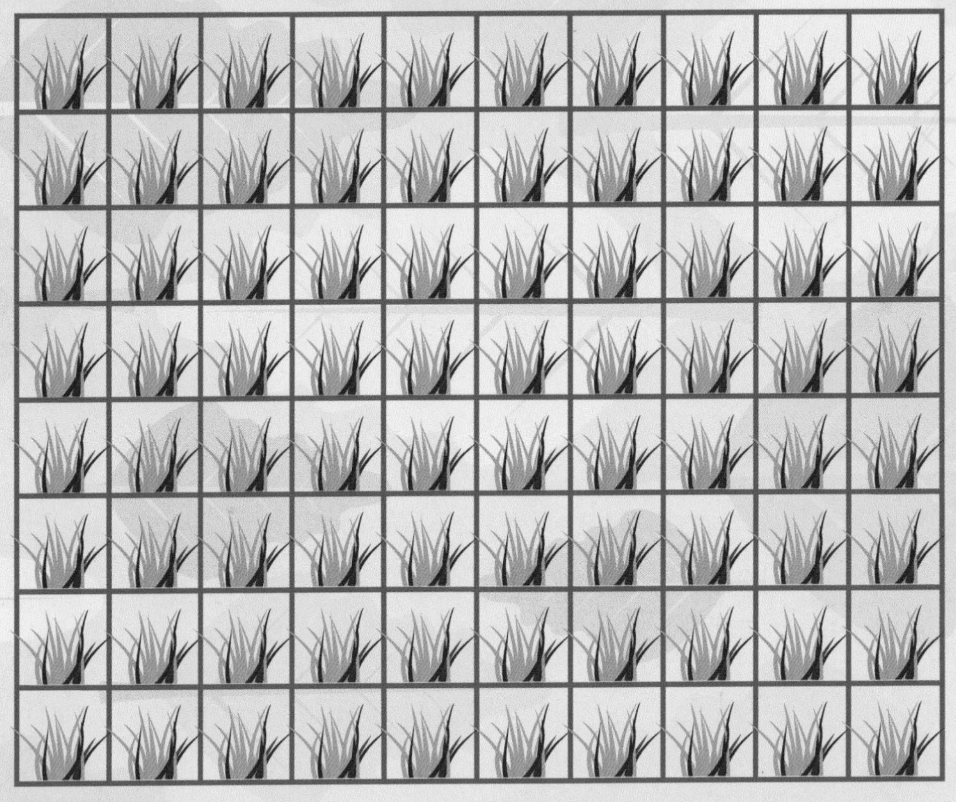

RULES: Hidden in this grid of tall grass are ten Pokémon! Take a pen, pencil, or crayon and mark off where you think the ten Pokémon are hiding. Check your score below to see how you did!

LEGEND

0–3 catches: You'll be awesome on our Pokémon team!

4–7 catches: You're doing really well! You'll be a Trainer in no time!

7–10 catches: Wow! Maybe you should head up a team of your own!

Turn to page 182 for the answers.

FIND THE DIFFERENCE

You've been doing well—now let's see if you can spot the difference between these Pokémon! Being a good Trainer means that you can tell an impostor Pokémon from a real one—test your skill at spotting which Pokémon isn't quite right! Check colors, body parts, expressions—anything that can make a difference! Good luck!

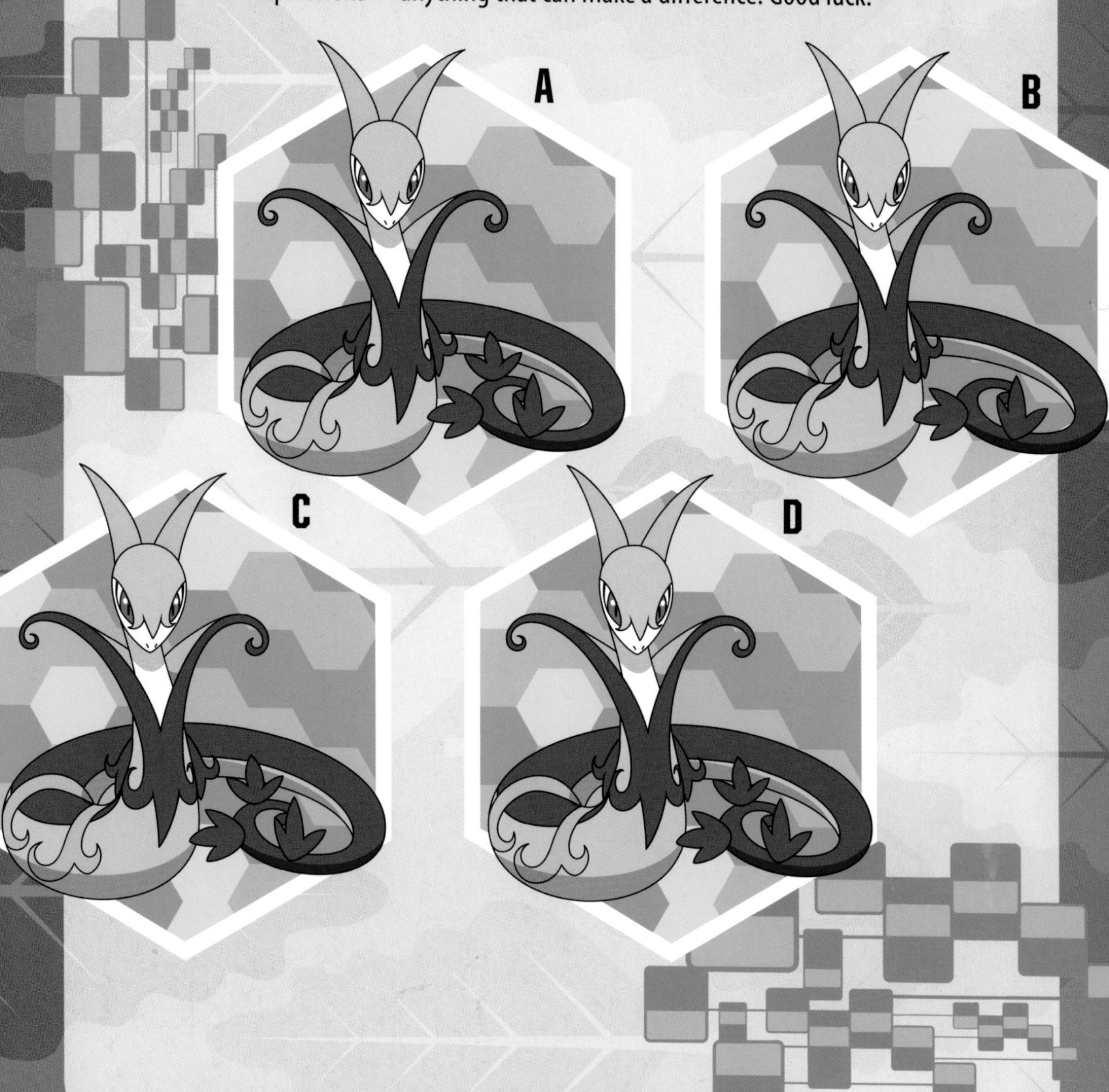

Turn to page 182 for the answer.

MATCH THE MOVE

It looks as if you're a natural as a Trainer. Can you match the Pokémon on the left below, with their moves on the right? Go on hotshot, show off your skills!

SUPERSONIC

GUST

STRING SHOT

Turn to page 182 for the answers.

POKÉMON SEEK AND FIND

Okay, we've tried this before. But, this time, see if you can pick out the two Grass-type Pokémon from the group of Pokémon shown. Remember—just the Grass types!

Turn to page 182 for the answers.

WATER TYPES

EVOLUTION REVOLUTION!

Okay, Trainer! Your knowledge of Water-type Pokémon is fantastic! It's time to see if you know about the possibilities of Pokémon progression, which is to say their Evolution! Guess what the next stage in your Pokémon's Evolution will be!

Turn to page 182 for the answer.

A PUZZLE OF POKÉMON

Let's see how well you can assemble the information at hand to help identify Pokémon—draw a line from each puzzle piece to where it should go in the puzzle!

A

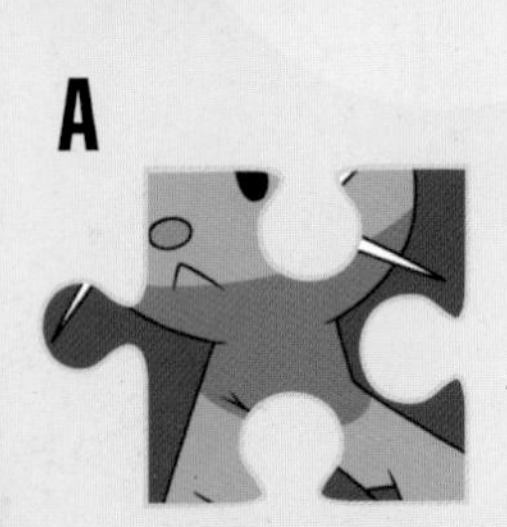

B

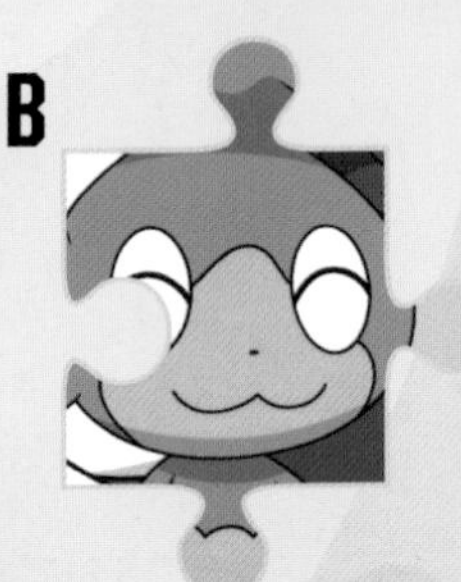

C

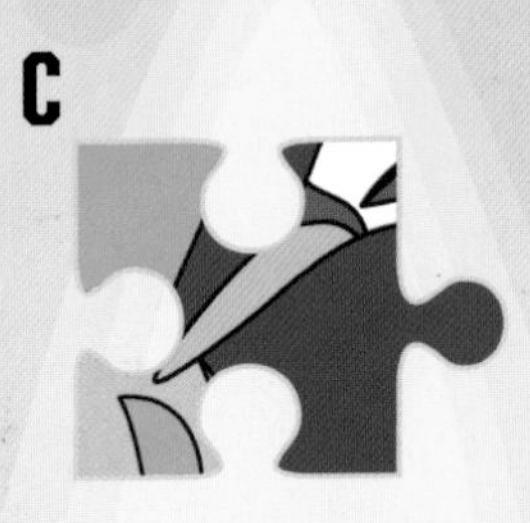

D

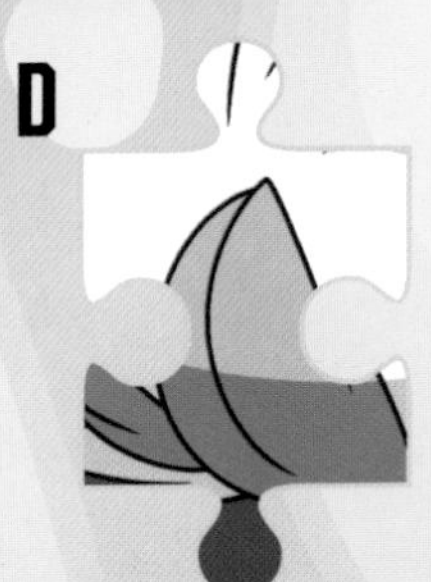

Turn to page 182 for the answers.

ODD POKÉMON OUT!

So many Pokémon, so many ways to catalog them! The Pokédex does a great job, but what happens when you're away from your equipment? Can you classify Pokémon using sight alone?

RULES: For this test, we're going to show you some different Pokémon. One of these Pokémon doesn't belong in the group, but which one? And what is the group? We'll give you three clues. You score yourself by how many clues you used!

CLUE #1: Almost everyone has another step ahead of them.

CLUE #2: Then again, some don't!

CLUE #3: No Evolution for you!

SCORE

1 clue: Wow! Maybe you should head up a team of your own!

2 clues: You're doing really well! You'll be a Trainer in no time!

3 clues: You'll be awesome on our Pokémon team!

Turn to page 182 for the answers.

POKÉMON SUDOKU

Trainers should keep themselves sharp, both in mind and body—and Sudoku is a great way to keep your wits sharp! Use just the numbers 1–9. Each number can appear only one time in a row, column, and box. Go to it, Trainers!

		2	7	3		6	4	9
		1	2		9	7	5	
4	9	7	5	8	6	3		2
7	5			2	4		9	1
8		4	9	1	5	2		6
1	2			6	7		3	4
6		5	1	9		4	2	
9	4	3	6		2			7
	1	8	4		3	9	6	5

Turn to page 182 for the answers.

TYPE CAST!

Pokémon identification requires that a Trainer also know the type of Pokémon he or she is facing. This is extremely important when battling Pokémon, since type advantages can easily turn a battle! So, see if you can match the Pokémon on the left with their types on the right.

Turn to page 183 for the answers.

ELECTRIC TYPES

SIMPLY STUNNING!

How well do you know Electric types, Trainer? Let's see if you can answer a few questions about their habits, Evolutions, and moves. Zap these questions down, and you'll be charged for your next task! Watt are you waiting for?

ACROSS

5. Who was suspected of being behind the thunderstorm that caused Pikachu to lose a move?

8. This Ground- and Electric-type Pokémon does not evolve.

10. Joltik evolves into ___________.

11. Name one type that Electric types are strong against.

12. Zebstrika evolves from this Pokémon.

13. Watchog uses this Electric-type move when battling for Lenora.

DOWN

1. What type are Electric types weak against?

2. Who is Ash's constant companion?

3. What Electric-type move does Pikachu launch from its tail?

4. Name another type that Electric types are strong against.

6. Fill in the Evolution: ___________, Eelektrik, Eelektross.

7. What type of move did Pikachu lose during a mysterious thunderstorm?

9. Oshawott sometimes uses this item, attached to its chest, to deflect Electric-type moves.

11. Emolga is a dual type. It's an Electric type and what other type?

Turn to page 183 for the answers.

HAIKU

Sometimes a poem is the perfect way to say how you feel. The type of poem known as a haiku is a great way to tell your favorite Pokémon just what you're feeling. Fill in the blanks, and be as creative as you can be!

RULES: Haikus are composed of three lines, with five syllables in the first line, seven in the second line, and five in the last line. Try to match the syllable counts as you compose a beautiful haiku for your Pokémon!

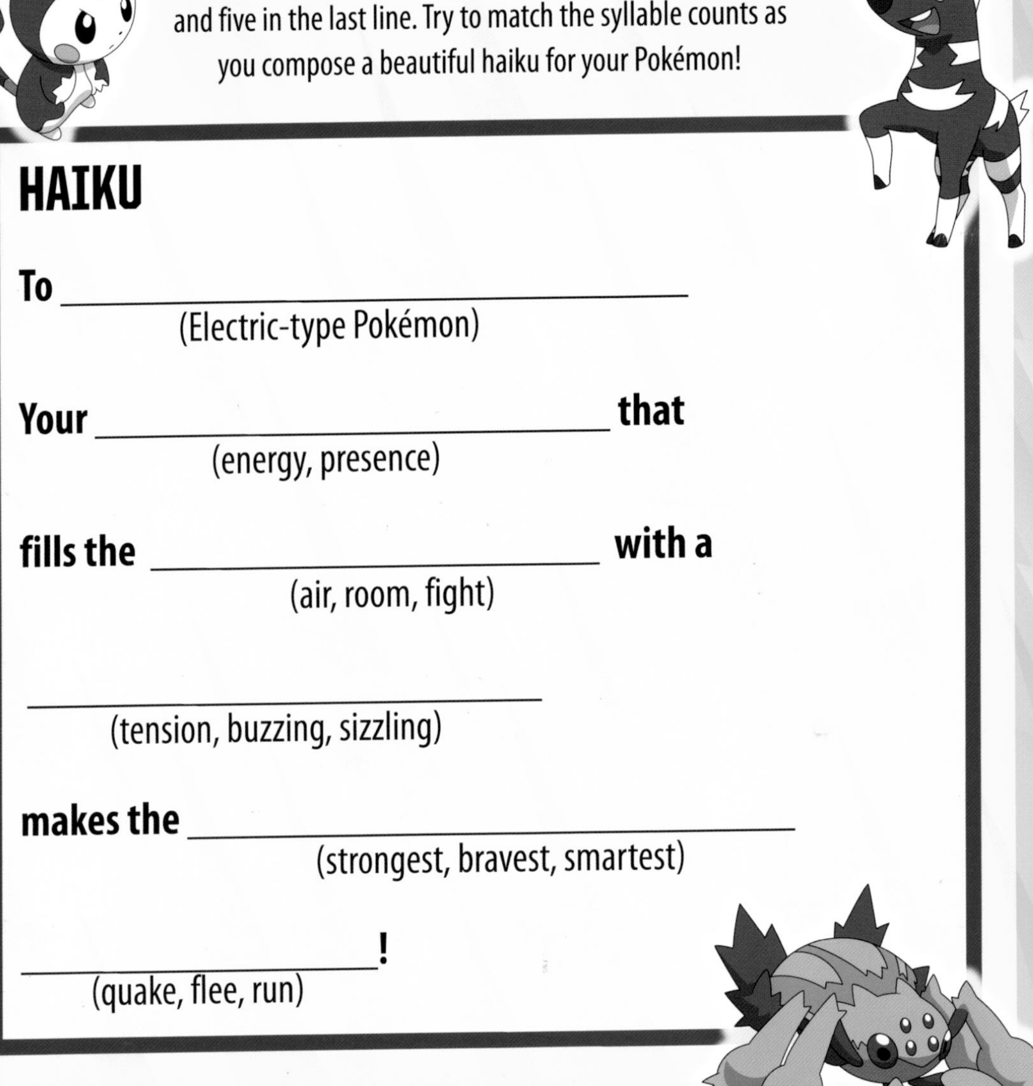

HAIKU

To ______________________________
(Electric-type Pokémon)

Your ________________________ **that**
(energy, presence)

fills the ____________________ **with a**
(air, room, fight)

____
(tension, buzzing, sizzling)

makes the ____________________________
(strongest, bravest, smartest)

________________**!**
(quake, flee, run)

WALL SCRAWL

Your adventure has led you to some clues about Pokémon in your area!
Other explorers seem to have left messages about the Pokémon they've seen.
Can you decipher these hastily worded scrawls?

Turn to page 183 for the answers.

AND THE WINNER IS...

Now's your chance to use your knowledge of Pokémon types in a real battle situation! Which of these Pokémon would have the advantage in battle? Use the <, >, or = symbols to show which Pokémon would have the upper hand (or leaf, or water spout, or tusk, as the case may be) in a matchup!

BASCULIN

GALVANTULA

CRYOGONAL

HAXORUS

REUNICLUS

MIENSHAO

Turn to page 183 for the answers.

FINISH THIS POKÉMON!

Well done! You've passed a tricky series of challenges to see if you really know your Pokémon! Now, we're setting a challenge to find out if you can remember what you've seen! Below is a Pokémon—color it in, and make sure you keep it neat and tidy! No Trainer wants a sloppy-looking Pokémon!

Turn to page 183 for the answer.

TRAINER PAGES

IRIS

WHO'S YOUR FRIEND?

No one can be a Pokémon Trainer and travel through a new region alone! You need the help and skills of other Trainers as well! So you know your Pokémon—do you know the Trainers that helped you out? Check your knowledge of other Trainers in Unova by correctly identifying which Pokémon travel with this Trainer!

Iris is bold and is never shy about giving Ash any kind of criticism. She may be tough, but she's completely devoted to her Pokémon!

Turn to page 183 for the answers.

TRAVEL CHECKLIST

Are you ready to go out in the world and make your mark as a Trainer? Make sure you have a travel checklist handy. Which of the following items would you decide not to take with you?

A BAG TO CARRY EVERYTHING?

A PERSONAL COMPUTER?

POKÉ BALLS?

PAPERWORK?

YOUR FAVORITE POKÉMON?

A BEACH BALL?

Turn to page 183 for the answers.

DOTS WHAT I'M TALKING ABOUT!

Keep a sharp eye out, Pokémon adventurer—sometimes it may seem like your senses are playing tricks on you! Don't forget, a good Pokémon Trainer knows that sometimes things aren't what they seem. Look closely at this picture. See if you can spot the hidden Pokémon—we'll even give you a few clues!

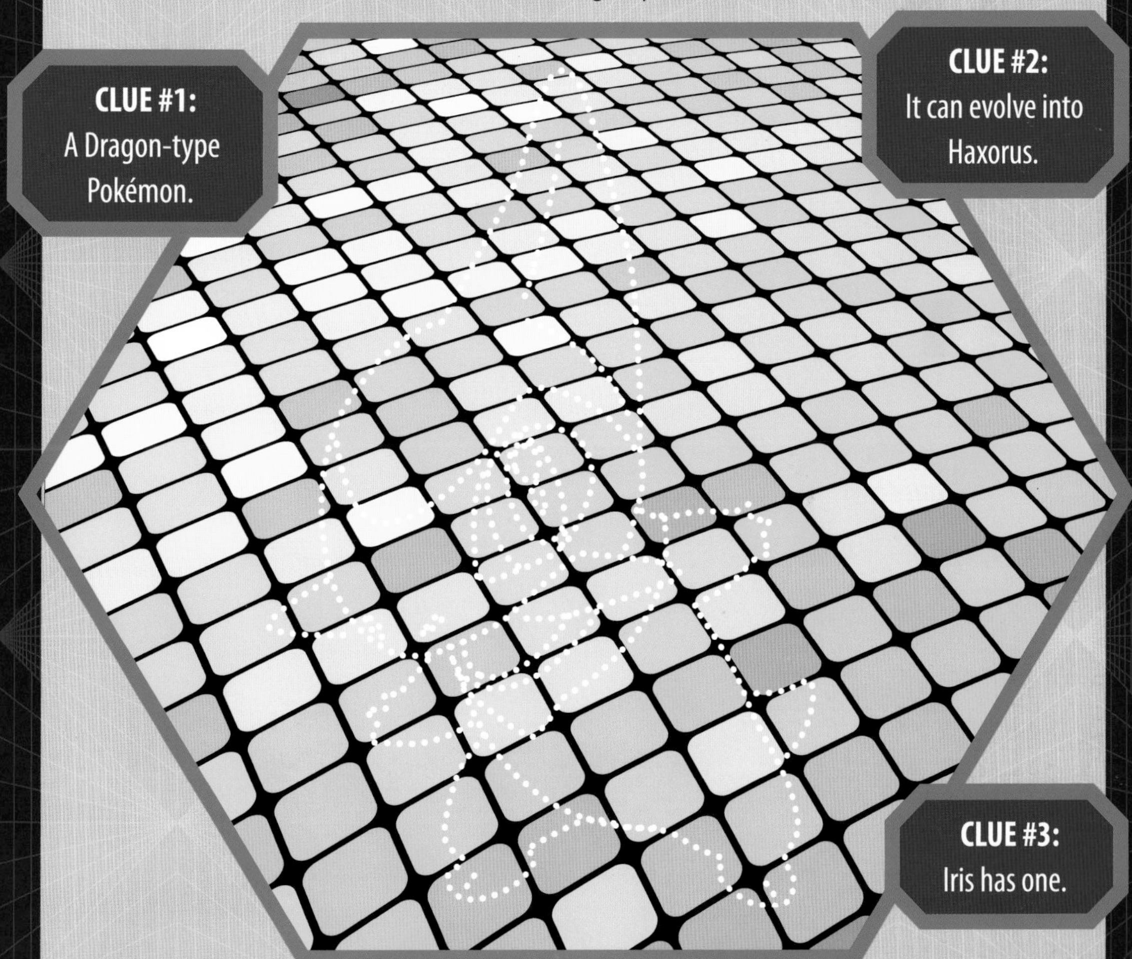

CLUE #1:
A Dragon-type Pokémon.

CLUE #2:
It can evolve into Haxorus.

CLUE #3:
Iris has one.

SCORE

1 clue: Wow! Maybe you should head up a team of your own!

2 clues: You're doing really well! You'll be a Trainer in no time!

3 clues: You'll be awesome on our Pokémon team!

Turn to page 183 for the answer.

SHAPE SHIFTING

Well, well, you're progressing quite nicely! Let's see if you've lost any of your visual skills—they're really important if you want to be a great Pokémon Trainer!

You see a shadow near a woodland meadow. Could those shapes be Pokémon hiding in the trees and grasses along a stream? Are those shapes just playing tricks on your eyes, or are they actually Pokémon? See if you can match these silhouettes to the Pokémon they belong to! Draw a line from the outline to the Pokémon it looks like. Good luck!

Turn to page 183 for the answers.

THE POKÉMON NAME GAME

Speed means a lot to a Trainer! Identifying your Pokémon and knowing their capabilities immediately is a key component of your training. Here's a one-, two-, or multi-player word game that tests how quick you are with your Pokémon.

RULES: You and a friend pick out a Unova Pokémon. Each of you then writes that Pokémon's name down on a piece of paper. Now, come up with as many words as you can from the letters in that Pokémon's name, within a two-minute time limit! The player with the most words wins!

EXAMPLE:

DRUDDIGON

1. Dud
2. Gird
3. Dun
4. Rug
5. Dig
6. Did
7. Rid
8. Don

BONUS

Use the memory cards in the back of this book. Flip them face down, then pick one card and use the Pokémon on that card as your choice. If you pick a Dragon-type Pokémon, you score a five-point bonus!

CRYPTOGLYPHICS

Can you decipher the following coded message? Use the clues from the Pokémon that we've found so far. . .

As _ _ _ _ finds out with both _ _ _ _ _ and _ _ _ _ _ _ _ _,

sometimes you _ _ _ _ _ _ the

_ _ _ _ _ _ _, and sometimes

the _ _ _ _ _ _ _ chooses you!

LEGEND

 = G

 = H

 = M

 = O

= P

 = R

 = S

 = T

 = W

Turn to page 183 for the answers.

KNOWLEDGE BASE

It's time for some more questions to test the Trainer in you! Can you get a perfect score?

1) Where does Iris meet Ash?

a) Outside Nuvema Town
b) Accumula Town
c) Nacrene City

2) Iris constantly tells Ash, "You're such a little ____."

a) Brat
b) Punk
c) Kid

3) What is the first Pokémon we see traveling with Iris?

a) Oshawott
b) Snivy
c) Axew

4) Iris believes the Nacrene City Museum is ________.

a) Open
b) Closed
c) Cursed

5) Who captures Emolga?

a) Ash
b) Cilan
c) Iris

6) When the Egg in Ash's party finally hatches, Iris tells Axew it will soon be a big _____.

a) Father
b) Brother
c) Man

7) Iris and Axew collect ________ to cure Scraggy after Galvantula attacked it.

a) Berries
b) Herbs
c) Plants

8) Iris and Axew find the perfect battling partner in __________.

a) Pikachu
b) Snivy
c) Scraggy

Turn to page 183 for the answers.

WORD SCRAMBLE

Some Pokémon are hard to understand. A very good Trainer knows that to uncover the heart of a Pokémon, communication is the key. That's why it's important for you to practice by deciphering the following Pokémon word scramble.

RULES: Unscramble each word. In the letters that form that word, there is a secret letter that is surrounded by a box. Those letters will spell out the answer!

QUESTION

Among other things, what is Iris's Emolga?

1. One of Lenora's Pokémon.

PLIULLIP _ _ _ _ ☐ _ _ _

2. Purrloin evolves into this.

PIDLEAR _ _ _ _ _ ☐ _

3. Iris has this Pokémon.

CAXEDLIRL _ _ _ _ _ ☐ _ _ _

4. Ash catches this Pokémon in Pinwheel Forest.

DAWSEDEL _ ☐ _ _ _ _ _ _

5. The city with a trio of Gym Leaders.

ATSNORIT ☐ _ _ _ _ _ _ _

6. Ash's rival.

PIRT _ _ ☐ _

7. Nacrene City has one.

SMEMUU _ _ ☐ _ _ _

8. Team Rocket has one in their party.

TWOBOA _ _ _ _ _ ☐

9. One of the three brothers running Striaton City Gym.

IILHC _ _ _ _ ☐

10. The Rock Hermit Pokémon.

BELDWBE _ _ _ ☐ _ _ _

11. The professor who helps find Musharna.

NEFNLE _ _ _ _ _ ☐

12. Lenora's husband.

SHWAE _ _ _ ☐ _

ANSWER

☐☐☐☐☐☐☐☐☐☐☐☐

Turn to page 183 for the answers.

COMPLETING THE TRAINER HELPS COMPLETE YOUR TRAINING!

Sometimes, being a Trainer means interacting with the other Trainers in your region. Ash has his hands full with the brash and outspoken Iris, a girl he meets on his adventures in Unova. Fill in the rest of Iris's Trainer outfit and see how accurate you can be!

Turn to page 183 for the answer.

POKÉMON ACROSTICS!

Let's play a game to help you get to know your Pokémon. This is a fun game that can be played with one, two, or multiple players.

RULES: Pick a Pokémon name. Write that name in a column. If you picked Emolga, you should have a puzzle that looks like this:

Now, try to spell the longest word you can with the letters in each row. For example, starting with the first row, try to spell a word that starts with E, but is very long—like energize! You can only make one word per row, but you get one point for each letter used. Try for the longest word you know!

BONUS

Time the game—see how many words you can come up with in two minutes!

BONUS

Use the memory cards in the back of this book. Flip them face down, then pick one card and use the Pokémon on that card as your choice. If you pick a Dragon-type Pokémon, you score a five-point bonus!

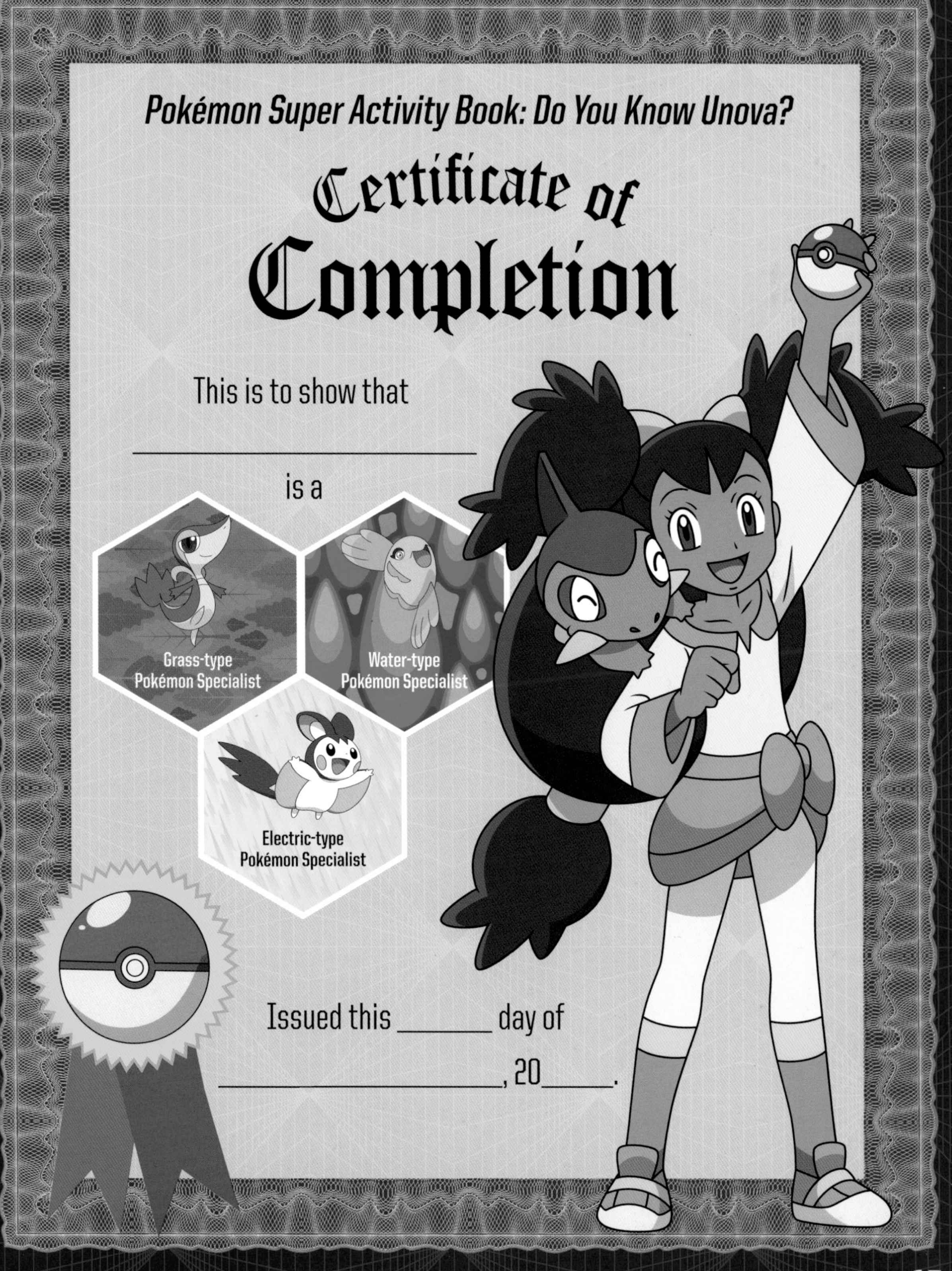
Pokémon Super Activity Book: Do You Know Unova?
Certificate of Completion
This is to show that
is a
Grass-type Pokémon Specialist
Water-type Pokémon Specialist
Electric-type Pokémon Specialist
Issued this ______ day of
____________________, 20_____.

POKÉMON
FUN TIME!

WHAT'S IN THE POKÉ BALL?

During your adventures in Unova, you have found a Poké Ball that another Trainer accidentally left behind at a Pokémon Center. The Trainer left some notes about the contents of the Poké Ball, but forgot to write down the Pokémon's name! See if you can guess which Pokémon is in the ball just from the clues!

SCORING

See how fast you can figure out what's in the Poké Ball! Score is based on how many clues you use!

1–3 clues: Wow! Maybe you should head up a team of your own!

4–7 clues: You're doing really well! You'll be a Trainer in no time!

8–9 clues: You'll be awesome on our Pokémon team!

CLUES

1. Fire type.

2. The Blazing Pokémon.

3. Try Zen Mode.

4. Evolved form.

5. Has two modes—Standard and Zen.

6. Knows Psychic-type moves.

7. Powerful, strong, and determined.

8. Starts with a "D".

9. Evolves from Darumaka.

Turn to page 183 for the answer.

POKÉ BALL MATCHUP

Did you know that there are many different kinds of Poké Balls? Some are better than others at catching Pokémon, depending on the Pokémon's type or location. See if you can match the Poké Ball with the Pokémon it will be most effective at catching!

NEST BALL
Works best on weaker Pokémon.

PATRAT

DIVE BALL
Works well on Pokémon near or in watery areas.

WOOBAT

NET BALL
Works well on Bug- and Water-type Pokémon.

DUSK BALL
Works better on Pokémon at night, or in dark places such as caves.

Turn to page 183 for the answers.

WHAT KIND OF TRAINER ARE YOU?

Let's get you ready for your great adventure! Fill in this info card to let us know how you're doing so far. Once you've filled it out, draw the equipment that you think you'll need on your trip!

My name is________________________.

I have a team of six Pokémon. They are:

1. ____
2. ____
3. ____
4. ____
5. ____
6. ____

The Pokémon I most want to catch is ________________________.

I am hoping to catch ____________________-type Pokémon the most.

My original hometown is ____________________________.

I am ________ years old.

My favorite Pokémon is _______________________________.

I am carrying the following in my backpack:

- ❑ Xtransceiver
- ❑ Pokédex: Caught: ______________ Seen: ______________
- ❑ Poké Balls: ____________________
- ❑ Berries
- ❑ Other: ________________

SAY WHAT?

The following has been heard around Unova.
Can you identify who said it?

"I'm a Pokémon Connoisseur!"

"If we travel together, I have no doubt the journey will be full of flavor."

"You're such a little kid!"

"From Pallet Town? Kanto region? See, I was just thinking that a guy like you came from the boonies."

"So, from now on, we both think you should call it Dragon Sneeze."

"See, back where I come from, it's a quiet little village where they specialize in raising Dragon-type Pokémon."

"Tepig, are you ready to train super-hard?"

"Okay, is this some kind of strategy? Calling moves that you can't even use?"

Turn to page 183 for the answers.

WHO AM I?

You'll meet lots of people on your journey—and you'll find it takes skill and patience to remember everyone's name! There are key people that you simply cannot ignore, people who are vital to your adventure. See if you can identify who this person is!

CLUE #1: Caring.

CLUE #2: Will help everyone in your party.

CLUE #3: Has identical sisters in nearly every town.

CLUE #4: Offers room and board.

CLUE #5: Rest here.

CLUE #6: Can be found in almost every town.

CLUE #7: Every Trainer's friend.

CLUE #8: Audino is her assistant.

CLUE #9: Is found in every Pokémon Center.

CLUE #10: Heals Pokémon.

SCORE

1–3 clues: Wow! Maybe you should head up a team of your own!
4–7 clues: You're doing really well! You'll be a Trainer in no time!
8–10 clues: You'll be awesome on our Pokémon team!

Turn to page 183 for the answer.

SHOW YOUR COLORS!

Get creative and show your Pokémon how proud of them you are! Create your own Pokémon flag to wave whenever you see your Pokémon!

STEP ONE: Draw your favorite Pokémon.

STEP TWO: Add symbols that represent your Pokémon (Fire-type, Water-type, Grass-type, etc.).

STEP THREE: Color your flag in with any colors that you think represent your Pokémon!

BATTLE PLAN

Coming up with a strategy to battle against an unfamiliar opponent is tough—and it's even tougher when your opponent switches out his or her Pokémon! In this test, you pick three Pokémon to battle the team below. Each of the opposing Pokémon has three moves it can use.

Ash has shown that type matchups don't always determine the winner—but they can still give you a real advantage in battle! If you need some tips for victory, try page 183!

YOUR TEAM:

SERVINE

Moves

a) Leer

b) Leaf Storm

c) Wrap

PIGNITE

Moves

a) Flame Charge

b) Arm Thrust

c) Tackle

DEWOTT

Moves

a) Razor Shell

b) Fury Cutter

c) Tail Whip

YOUR OPPONENT'S TEAM:

DWEBBLE

Moves

a) Rock Blast

b) Fury Cutter

c) Bug Bite

DRILBUR

Moves

a) Dig

b) Drill Run

c) Metal Claw

HERDIER

Moves

a) Bite

b) Take Down

c) Giga Impact

LIGHTS! CAMERA! POKÉMON!

Ever dream of making your very own Pokémon movie? Well, now you can, with this Pokémon Movie Maker! Simply add in the names of the characters you'd like to see, the Pokémon you'd like to direct, and the towns and situations you'd like to experience. Great job, Trainer!

MY POKÉMON MOVIE TITLE: ______________________________

The Pokémon I would like to see in my movie:

1. ____________________
2. ____________________
3. ____________________
4. ____________________
5. ____________________
6. ____________________
7. ____________________
8. ____________________

The Trainers I would like to see:

1. ____________________
2. ____________________
3. ____________________
4. ____________________

The places I would visit:

1. ____________________
2. ____________________
3. ____________________
4. ____________________

The situation I would resolve:

1. Someone is trying to take all the Pokémon away!
2. Someone is trying to use mind control on the Trainers!
3. Someone is trying to use Pokémon for their own personal gain!

WHODUNIT?

A Pokémon has recently been through this area, and you have to use your superior Trainer skills to help the people here figure out which Pokémon it was. Can you guess the identity of the Pokémon by studying the clues it left behind?

WHODUNIT?

You see a bare patch of grass, burnt to a crisp. This patch of grass is next to a mansion that has reportedly been haunted for years. People in these parts have complained that, at night, ghostly Pokémon can sometimes be seen glowing faintly in the mansion's windows. The Pokémon that burned the grass must be a Ghost type as well. As you peek in the windows, you spot the ___________ looking back at you!

WHODUNIT?

In the tall grass of the plains, you see hoof marks that have beaten a large path through the grass. You follow the marks and hear a strange whinnying sound. You feel the hair rising on the back of your neck. You notice a small Blitzle running around near the horizon, and you realize that you must have angered the head of the herd. You turn, right into the path of an angry _______________!

WHODUNIT?

Somewhere in the heart of a dusty museum, a Pokémon roams the deserted hallways, looking for its mask. The people in this museum had no right to take the mask from this Pokémon—although you suspect that they didn't do it on purpose. This Pokémon passes the suits of armor and decides to inhabit one, just to see if it can get anyone's attention. It's tough being a ghost. You have also heard that another of its kind was captured by Team Rocket… It's a ________________.

Turn to page 183 for the answers.

DRAGON TYPES

WORD SEARCH—DRAGON!

Calling all Trainers! Dragon-type Pokémon are one of the trickier types to train. They can be elusive, powerful, and very, very aggressive. Do you have the mettle to master these mighty Pokémon? See if you can spot the Dragon types in this word search.

C	E	D	E	I	N	O	F	T	Y	R	B	F	L	O	L	W	A	A	F	G	E	W	D	D
V	A	M	R	L	C	Q	M	M	D	Z	Q	H	E	R	D	I	E	R	N	P	U	A	T	U
A	I	P	C	D	M	R	Y	G	C	O	Q	E	A	K	R	N	Y	P	C	R	S	C	B	U
X	G	H	E	F	R	A	X	U	R	E	V	B	E	N	U	C	O	X	D	A	F	Y	V	B
E	L	N	Y	D	X	O	N	O	Z	O	Z	X	O	H	D	U	R	V	D	X	V	Z	N	N
O	D	K	F	Y	R	D	D	V	D	O	V	G	V	I	D	N	O	K	Z	I	A	D	M	G
S	T	M	O	A	G	Y	L	I	L	L	I	P	U	P	I	L	E	F	N	A	X	E	F	Q
H	Y	P	A	W	V	Y	P	R	Q	E	H	Q	N	G	G	T	L	S	D	Y	E	E	E	E
A	H	E	P	Y	M	B	Y	W	R	W	W	D	I	R	O	F	R	P	S	J	W	R	Y	H
W	Q	D	D	X	T	Q	Q	D	L	D	C	P	C	C	N	A	R	E	W	Q	Q	L	P	U
O	M	Y	R	M	P	W	Y	X	W	R	E	R	Q	M	H	J	U	C	S	T	L	I	W	X
T	L	B	R	E	E	H	S	P	A	T	R	A	T	A	P	L	C	L	Y	E	P	N	K	L
T	I	C	L	F	I	T	K	Z	W	E	I	L	O	U	S	X	R	C	A	H	R	G	M	M
F	P	X	Y	Q	H	A	X	O	R	U	S	E	I	M	C	W	A	T	C	H	O	G	J	M
A	T	R	E	C	O	E	B	L	X	G	U	A	F	D	Q	L	T	S	W	J	D	T	M	Y

Turn to page 183 for the answers.

POKÉMON FINDER

Okay, it's time to train your inner eye to spot a Pokémon! Hidden deep in these caves are elusive Dragon-type Pokémon. Can you throw a Poké Ball with accuracy? Can you rely on your instinct to find the hidden Pokémon? Good luck!

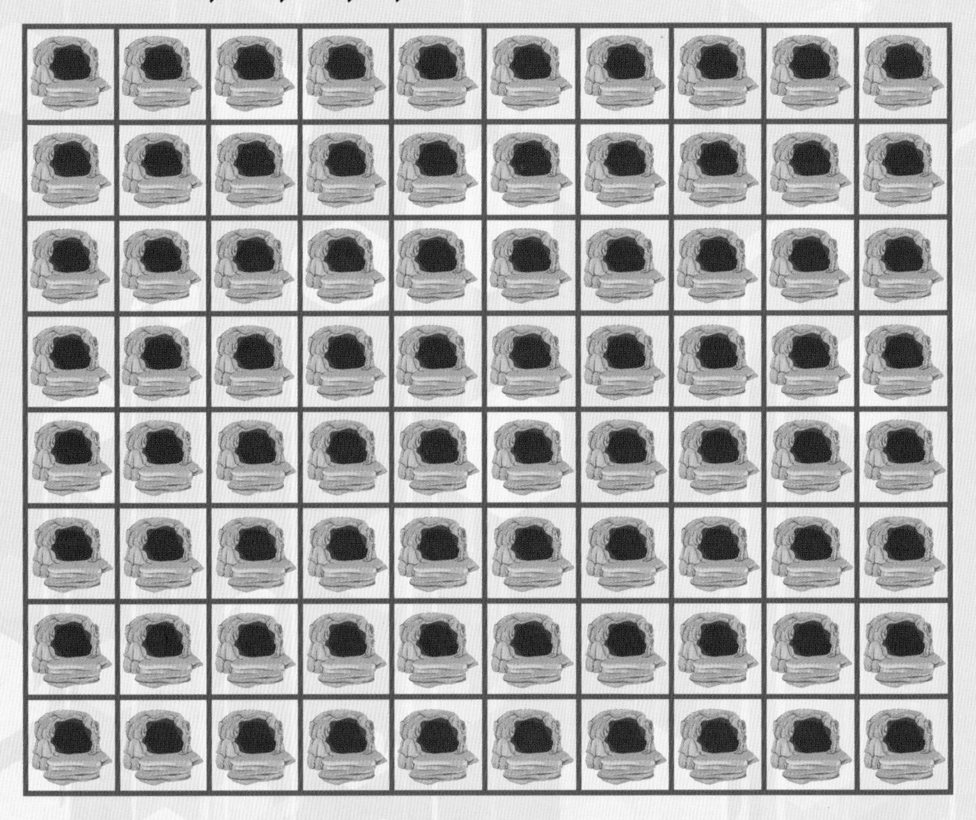

RULES: Hidden in this grid of caves are ten Pokémon! Take a pen, pencil, or crayon and mark off where you think the ten Pokémon are hiding. Check your score below to see how you did!

LEGEND

0–3 catches: You'll be awesome on our Pokémon team!

4–7 catches: You're doing really well! You'll be a Trainer in no time!

7–10 catches: Wow! Maybe you should head up a team of your own!

Turn to page 184 for the answers.

FIND THE DIFFERENCE

All right! Nice job spotting the Dragon-type Pokémon! Now, let's see how skilled you are at spotting which of these Pokémon is the imposter! In this lineup of four Axew, one is definitely not like the others. Can you find the one that isn't quite right? Be careful—Dragon types don't always let you get this close to inspect them!

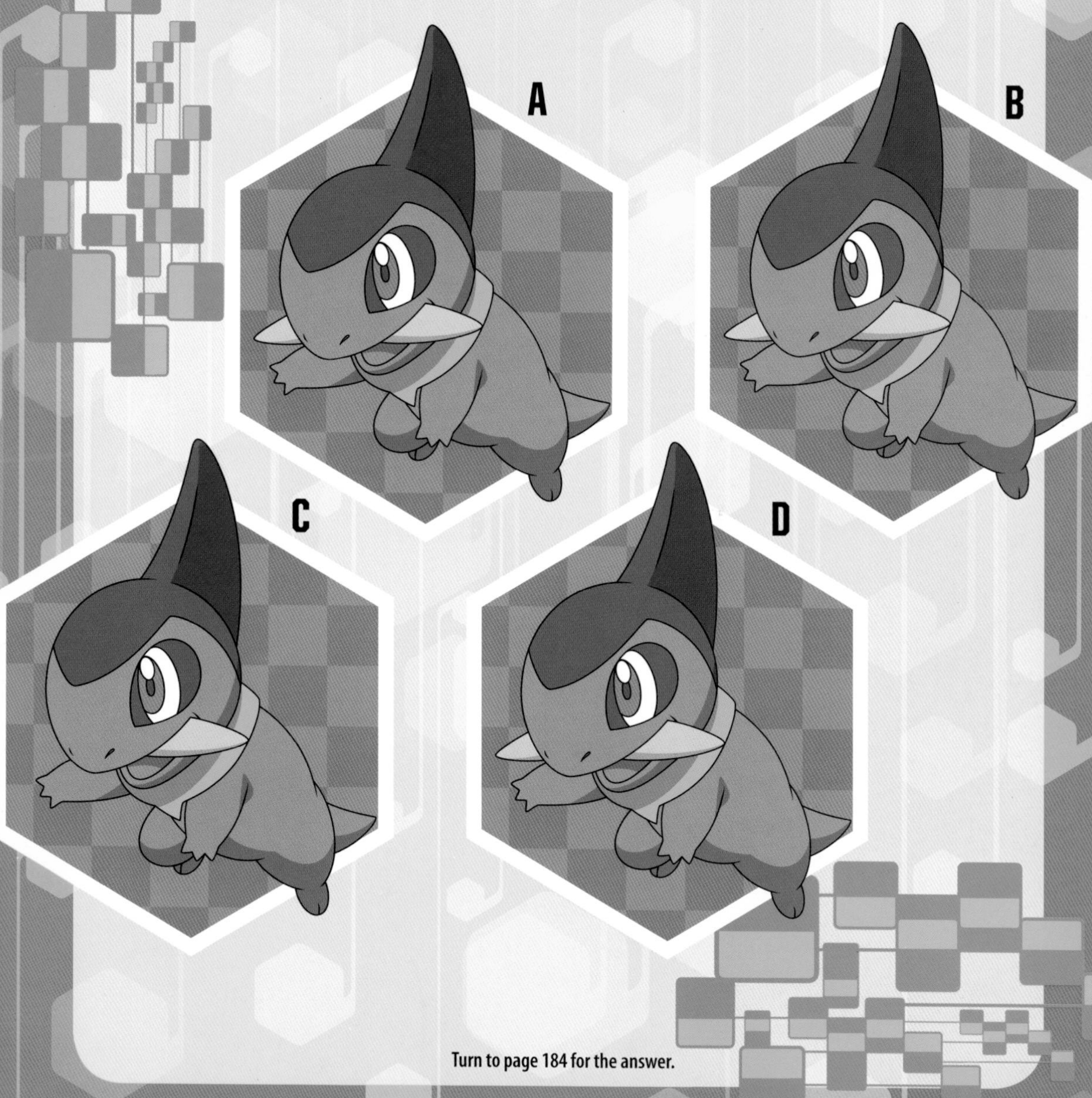

Turn to page 184 for the answer.

MATCH THE MOVE

You may be a great Trainer in the making, but there is always more to learn! Let's start by matching the Pokémon on the left with their moves on the right. It's time to show off just how knowledgeable you really are!

METAL CLAW

AIR SLASH

DRAGON RAGE

Turn to page 184 for the answers.

POKÉMON SEEK AND FIND

Okay, quick—visual identification of Pokémon needs to get under way! Limit yourself to Dragon types. There are three in this collage. Proceed!

Turn to page 184 for the answers.

STEEL TYPES

EVOLUTION REVOLUTION!

Wow, Dragon types proved to be a real challenge! Let's move on to Steel-type Pokémon and see if you can spot their Evolutions with just as much skill. Pick out the Pokémon that fills the gap in the following Pokémon Evolutions:

Turn to page 184 for the answers.

A PUZZLE OF POKÉMON

Let's see how well you can assemble the information at hand to help identify Pokémon—draw a line from each puzzle piece to where it should go in the puzzle!

Turn to page 184 for the answers.

ODD POKÉMON OUT!

Let's put a group of Pokémon on the page, and see if you can tell why one of these does not belong with the others. We'll even throw in some clues, but we know you don't need them. Which one of these Pokémon does not belong here?

RULES: For this test, we're going to show you some different Pokémon. One of these Pokémon doesn't belong in the group, but which one? And what is the group? We'll give you three clues. You score yourself by how many clues you used!

CLUE #1: Some Pokémon won't change.

CLUE #2: Forget about Evolution.

CLUE #3: One of these Pokémon still has a ways to go.

SCORE

1 clue: Wow! Maybe you should head up a team of your own!

2 clues: You're doing really well! You'll be a Trainer in no time!

3 clues: You'll be awesome on our Pokémon team!

Turn to page 184 for the answers.

POKÉMON SUDOKU

Trainers should keep themselves sharp, both in mind and body—
and Sudoku is a great way to keep your wits sharp! Use just the numbers 1–9.
Each number can appear only one time in a row, column, and box. Go to it, Trainers!

5	4		7	3	2		6	
7		9	6	1		5	3	4
3		8		9	4		1	
9	8		4	2	6	3		1
	5	3		7	1		9	
2	1	4			9	7		6
	3		1	6		8	7	9
1	9	5	2	8	7	6		3
8	7	6		4	3		2	5

Turn to page 184 for the answers.

TYPE CAST!

When battling, knowing the type of Pokémon you're facing is hugely important—it can mean the difference in winning or losing the fight. When you know what you're facing, you can make sure to send the right type of Pokémon out! See if you can match the Pokémon on the left with its type on the right.

Turn to page 184 for the answers.

GHOST TYPES

BOO!

It's time to test your knowledge of specific Pokémon types.
Let's try a little crossword to sharpen your Ghost-type Pokémon skills.

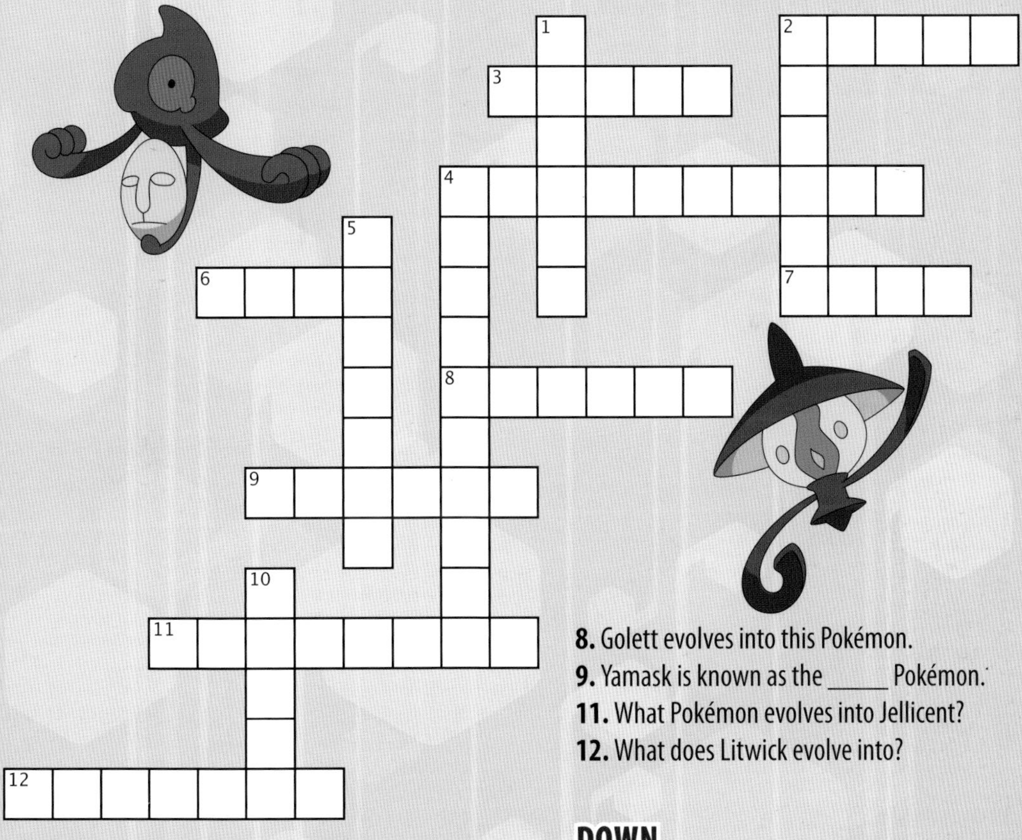

ACROSS

2. This is one of the types that is most effective against Ghost types.

3. What is the name of the Co-Curator of the Nacrene City Museum?

4. What is the final Evolution of Litwick?

6. Who was the Trainer that was convinced the Nacrene City Museum was haunted?

7. What is another type that Ghost types are effective against?

8. Golett evolves into this Pokémon.

9. Yamask is known as the _____ Pokémon.

11. What Pokémon evolves into Jellicent?

12. What does Litwick evolve into?

DOWN

1. This Pokémon haunted Hawes.

2. Golurk is a dual type. It's a Ghost type and what other type?

4. Another "relic" that was on display in the Nacrene City Museum.

5. One of the types that Ghost types are most effective against.

10. Name the Trainer who doubted the Nacrene City Museum was haunted.

Turn to page 184 for the answers.

HAIKU

You're proving to be the best Trainer we've seen in a long time! Your close relationship with your Pokémon is gaining you a lot of recognition. Let's see if you can continue to impress by writing a short poem to your Ghost-type Pokémon!

RULES: Haikus are composed of three lines, with five syllables in the first line, seven in the second line, and five in the last line. Try to match the syllable counts to compose a beautiful haiku for your Pokémon!

HAIKU

To ______________________________
(Ghost-type Pokémon)

You _______________, **and** _______________________
(float, fly, lurk) (sighing, moving, flitting)

sense ____________________________
(trouble, something, danger)

all ______________________ **me.**
(about, around, within)

Thank you for _________________________.
(caring, watching, knowing)

WALL SCRAWL

Your adventure has led you to some clues about Pokémon in your area! Other explorers seem to have left messages about the Pokémon they've seen. Can you decipher these hastily worded scrawls?

Turn to page 184 for the answers.

HELP FRILLISH!

Frillish has lost its way, and needs to get back to Trip as quickly as it can! Help Frillish navigate its way as it tries to reconnect with its Trainer!

Turn to page 184 for the answer.

FINISH THIS POKÉMON!

Can you remember what the different colors of a Pokémon look like? You're a Trainer, so you should be able to correctly color this Pokémon using only your memory. You should have no trouble at all, right? Good luck! See if you know your Pokémon as well as you think you do!

Turn to page 184 for the answer.

PIECE OF MINE

Your last visual test, Trainer! Can you tell which piece of the Pokémon is highlighted? Match the Pokémon pieces with the Pokémon to which they belong. Be alert! Ghost types are shy and rarely seen, so you'll have to look carefully.

Turn to page 184 for the answers.

FIND THE DIFFERENCE

Dragon and Steel types didn't seem to faze you—so let's take a quick round to see if you can spot the Ghost-type Pokémon that's an imposter. The difference may be minor, but it's a major accomplishment to spot it!

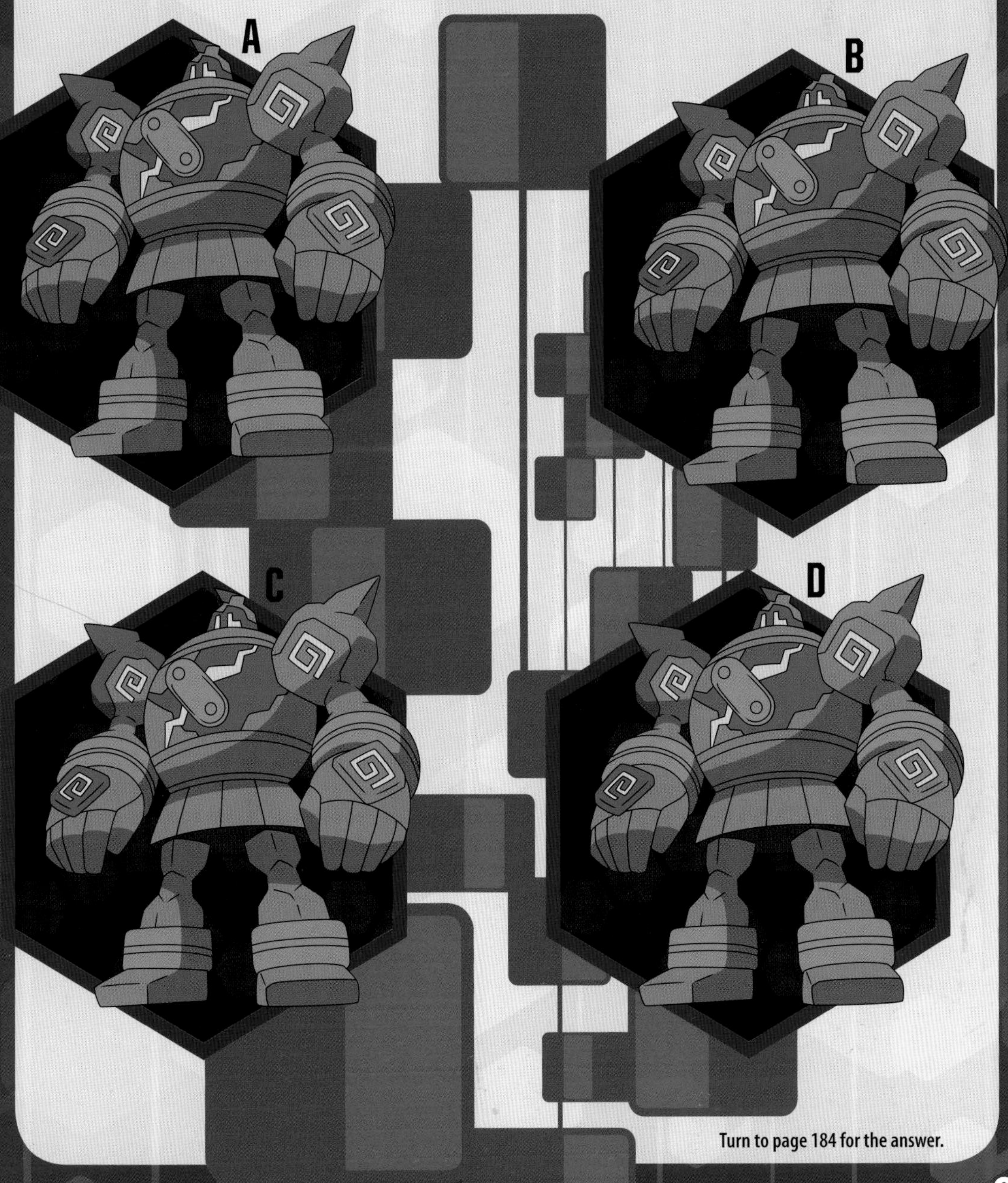

Turn to page 184 for the answer.

TRAINER PAGES

CILAN

WHO'S YOUR FRIEND?

You're really getting to know a lot of the Trainers in the Unova region. Let's see how well you know their Pokémon! You need this information, because sizing up an opponent and battling may require you to bring in some extra help—and it's always good to have a friend watch your back!

Cilan is a Pokémon Connoisseur, a refined gentleman who is just as passionate about his culinary talents as he is about his Pokémon! He knows how to soothe a friend beaten in battle, and he also knows how to assess when a battle will turn based on the relationship between a Trainer and his or her Pokémon. But Cilan doesn't really catch a lot of Pokémon himself. See if you can identify which Pokémon have accompanied him on his adventure through Unova!

Turn to page 184 for the answers.

TRAVEL CHECKLIST

Are you ready to go out in the world and make your mark as a Trainer? Make sure you have a travel checklist handy. Which of the following items would you decide not to take with you?

A LAWNMOWER?

A TENNIS RACKET?

A DRESS?

POKÉDEX?

A TELEVISION?

A CAR?

Turn to page 185 for the answers.

DOTS WHAT I'M TALKING ABOUT!

Seeing dots usually means a visit to the eye doctor, but not this time! Cleverly hidden Pokémon are using your eyes against you! They're hoping you don't see them camouflaged in the background. Look closely at this picture. See if you can spot the hidden Pokémon—we'll even give you a few clues!

CLUE #1: One of three Pokémon that the Striaton City Gym Leaders used

CLUE #3: Ash's first Pokémon

CLUE #3: Ash's first Pokémon battle with Cilan involved this Pokémon

SCORE

1 clue: Wow! Maybe you should head up a team of your own!

2 clues: You're doing really well! You'll be a Trainer in no time!

3 clues: You'll be awesome on our Pokémon team!

Turn to page 185 for the answer.

WHAT'S THAT? IS IT A POKÉMON?

So, how's your training going so far? Are your eyes sore? Are your hands cramping? Of course not, because Trainers are tough! Pokémon Trainers are not just tough, though—they're persistent! So, after a long day of catching Pokémon, you still have to be on top of your game.

What lurks in the rocks? Is there something in the trees? Can you see something deep in the bushes? Are those shapes just playing tricks on your eyes, or are they actually Pokémon? See if you can match these silhouettes to the Pokémon they belong to! Draw a line from the outline to the Pokémon it looks like. Good luck!

Turn to page 185 for the answers.

THE POKÉMON NAME GAME

When you're a Trainer, keeping yourself in shape mentally is just as important as keeping your body in shape physically! One way to do this is to figure out a puzzle like the one below. . .

RULES: You and a friend pick out a Unova Pokémon. Each of you then writes that Pokémon's name down on a piece of paper. Now, come up with as many words as you can from the letters in that Pokémon's name, within a two-minute time limit! The player with the most words wins!

EXAMPLE:

BONUS

Use the memory cards in the back of this book. Flip them face down, then pick one card and use the Pokémon on that card as your choice. If you pick a Grass-type Pokémon, you score a five-point bonus!

CRYPTOGLYPHICS

Can you decipher the following coded message?
Use the clues from the Pokémon that we've found so far...

 _  _ knows that the

 _  of life is in the

_ _  _   _ _ _  that you

battle with!

What _  _ _ comes from

sitting on the  _   _ _   ?

LEGEND

=A  =C  =E  =D  =G

=L  =O  =P =S =T

Turn to page 185 for the answers.

KNOWLEDGE BASE

A great Trainer knows everything about his or her opponent. So, let's test your knowledge! How well do you know Cilan? Can you answer every one of these questions right?

1. What city does Ash find Cilan in?

2. What are Cilan's battling brothers' names?

3. What does Cilan consider himself?

4. Which Pokémon does Cilan use when facing Ash for the first time?

5. A Pokémon hits Pansage in the head with what object, causing it to fall ill?

6. What type of Pokémon is Pansage?

7. Who is the other Connoisseur that the team meets?

8. Cilan catches another Pokémon after its shell gets stolen. What is this Pokémon?

9. What type or types is this Pokémon?

10. What function does Cilan perform for Ash's team?

Turn to page 185 for the answers.

WORD SCRAMBLE

A lot of training can be puzzling. You have to decipher a Pokémon's moods, its intentions, and even, at times, its behavior. A lot of the work involved in training your Pokémon is reading between the lines and sensing what your Pokémon wants or needs before it has to tell you.

RULES: Unscramble each word. In the letters that form that word, there are secret letters that are surrounded by a box. Those letters will spell out the answer!

QUESTION: What do you need when battling Pokémon and preparing fine food?

1. Cilan witnesses a battle between this and a Dewott at the Pokémon Battle Club.

RSIENVE _ _ _ ☐ _ _ _

2. The final Evolution of Tepig.

OABMRE _ _ _ _ ☐ _

3. Trip uses this Pokémon, which impresses Cilan.

SHFLRILI _ ☐ _ _ _ _ _ _

4. Bianca uses this Pokémon, which is the next Evolution of Tepig.

IIENPTG _ ☐ _ _ _ _ _

5. Iris uses this Pokémon, but it refuses to obey her for a while.

AEDXIRLLC ☐ _ _ _ _ _ _ _ _

6. Emolga and Axew infuriate a swarm of these in a forest.

TBWSOAO _ _ _ _ _ _ ☐

7. Before it's Cofagrigus, it's this Pokémon.

MSYKAA ☐ _ _ _ _ _

ANSWER ☐☐☐☐☐☐☐

Turn to page 185 for the answers.

COMPLETING THE TRAINER HELPS COMPLETE YOUR TRAINING!

Everyone should have a Pokémon Connoisseur along with them on their journey—they can smell the aroma of a bad matchup and suggest various ways to spice it up! Cilan is just that kind of Connoisseur. He's refined, helpful, and a great cook! See if you can color him in correctly to make sure that his skills stay fresh!

Turn to page 185 for the answer.

POKÉMON ACROSTICS!

Let's play a game to help you get to know your Pokémon.
This is a fun game that can be played with one, two, or multiple players.

RULES: Pick a Pokémon name. Write that name in a column.
If you picked Pansage, you should have a puzzle that looks like this:

Now, try to spell the longest word you can with the letters in each row. For example, starting with the first row, try to spell a word that starts with P, but is very long — like premonition! You can only make one word per row, but you get one point for each letter used. Try for the longest word you know!

BONUS

Time the game—see how many words you can come up with in two minutes!

BONUS

Use the memory cards in the back of this book. Flip them face down, then pick one card and use the Pokémon on that card as your choice. If you pick a Grass-type Pokémon, you score a five-point bonus!

Pokémon Super Activity Book:
Do You Know Unova?
Certificate of
Completion
This is to show that
is a
Dragon-type
Pokémon Specialist
Steel-type
Pokémon Specialist
Ghost-type
Pokémon Specialist
Issued this
day of ,
20 .

FLYING TYPES

WORD SEARCH—FLYING!

So, you're moving up the ranks, Pokémon Trainer! Good for you! We now move on to the speedy and powerful Flying types. Flying types are fast, and can use strong moves like Air Cutter and Aerial Ace. In the word search below, look for the Flying types, or dual Flying types, and leave everything else up in the air!

S A M U R O T T U E M O L G A W P I Y A H S O V M
E Z K I Z P I U W N S W A N N A L J Q F H F E A A
R F R U F F L E T G F R X U E P I N S J D E C L N
P Y K W Z E S S W C I E H A R C H E O P S E L U D
E W D D C B G I W O Q P Z P I K A C H U Z M V I I
R W E J D Y P G Z O O S E A E W Z Q K T K B V Y B
I A E T T L O I L A O B Q U N W U L B F U O U N U
O D V D P V K L D H M B A S T T C C R F M A L F Z
R J F S D L I Y I O R Y A T O A X R A B T R L G Z
L U K Q P U U P B S V T K T C R D S V P R B A O X
U W X U Q X C H I O W E W F K C N S I V O T B L N
B A D N V F Z W S R X P L A N H B A A O P L Y T U
Q Y A C D B H K C X M D S P Z E H L R X M Z Y R U
Y R U S X O P V K D G N B D T N D L Y S T I A H Q
T R Y G W D U C K L E T T K N R G F L H G F M G C

Turn to page 185 for the answers.

POKÉMON FINDER

Okay, so you know how to recognize a Pokémon by name!
Now let's see if you can catch Pokémon by instinct alone!

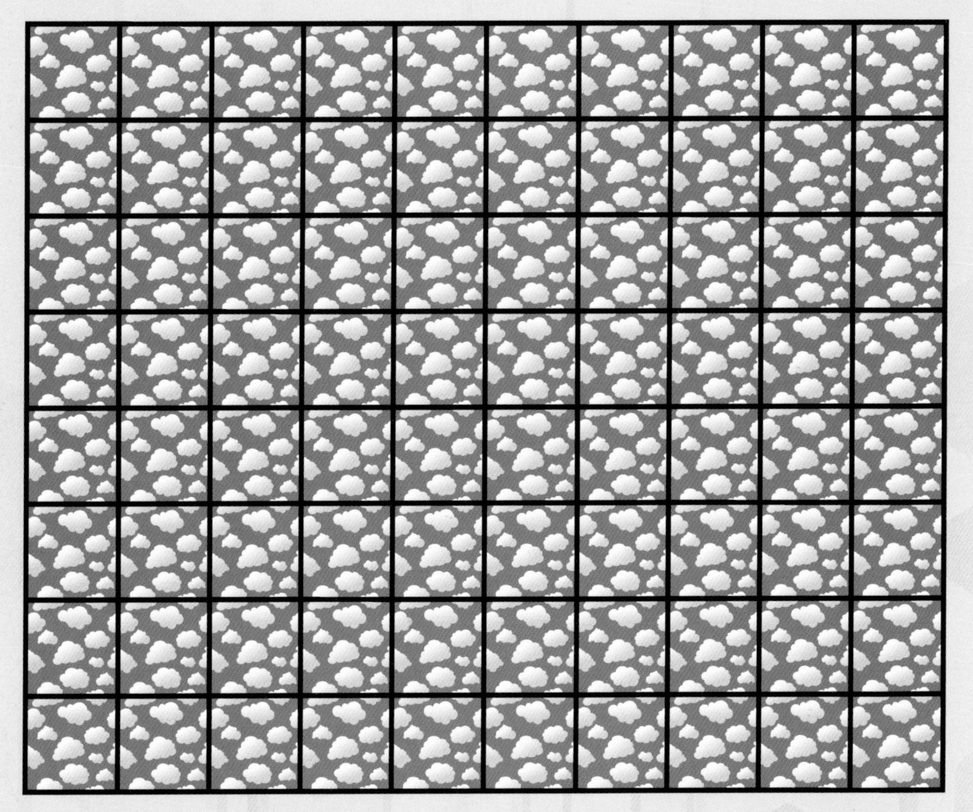

RULES: Hidden in this grid of clouds are ten Pokémon! Take a pen, pencil, or crayon and mark off where you think the ten Pokémon are hiding. Check your score below to see how you did!

LEGEND

0–3 catches: You'll be awesome on our Pokémon team!
4–7 catches: You're doing really well! You'll be a Trainer in no time!
7–10 catches: Wow! Maybe you should head up a team of your own!

Turn to page 185 for the answers.

FIND THE DIFFERENCE

Wow, you are really starting to shine, Trainer! Just a couple of more tests to get you certified as a Flying-type specialist. This one is crucial—can you spot which of these Pokémon is the imposter? Check colors, appendages, expressions—anything that can make a difference! Good luck!

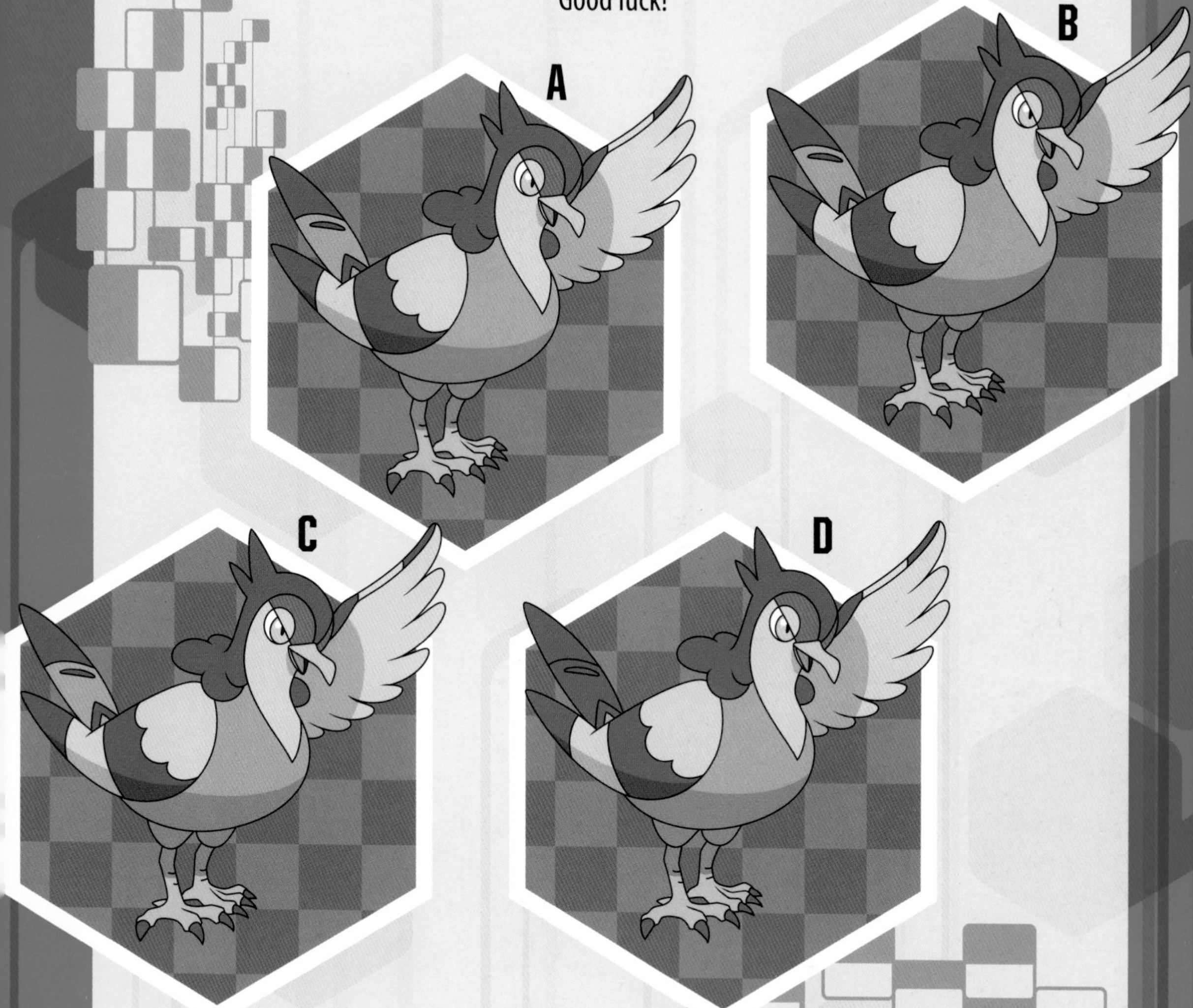

A

B

C

D

Turn to page 185 for the answer.

MATCH THE MOVE

You "flew" right through that last exercise. You really know your Flying types, don't you? Spotting the differences may not seem like much, but all Trainers have to know their Pokémon through and through! This also means studying their habits and behaviors, and—most importantly—their moves. Can you match the Pokémon on the left with their moves on the right?

BUBBLEBEAM

VOLT SWITCH

SKY ATTACK

Turn to page 185 for the answers.

POKÉMON SEEK AND FIND

So, you know your Pokémon? Find three Flying types in this collage of Unova Pokémon! That's it—quick and to the point!

Turn to page 185 for the answers.

POISON TYPES

EVOLUTION REVOLUTION!

Once again, excellent Pokémon recognition skills require you to know their appearance, their habitat, and their moves. Those same skills also require that you think ahead and know Pokémon Evolutions as well. Can you figure out which Pokémon is missing in this Evolution chain? If you guess correctly, you're on your way to greatness!

Turn to page 185 for the answer.

A PUZZLE OF POKÉMON

Let's see how well you can assemble the information at hand to help identify Pokémon—draw a line from each puzzle piece to where it should go in the puzzle!

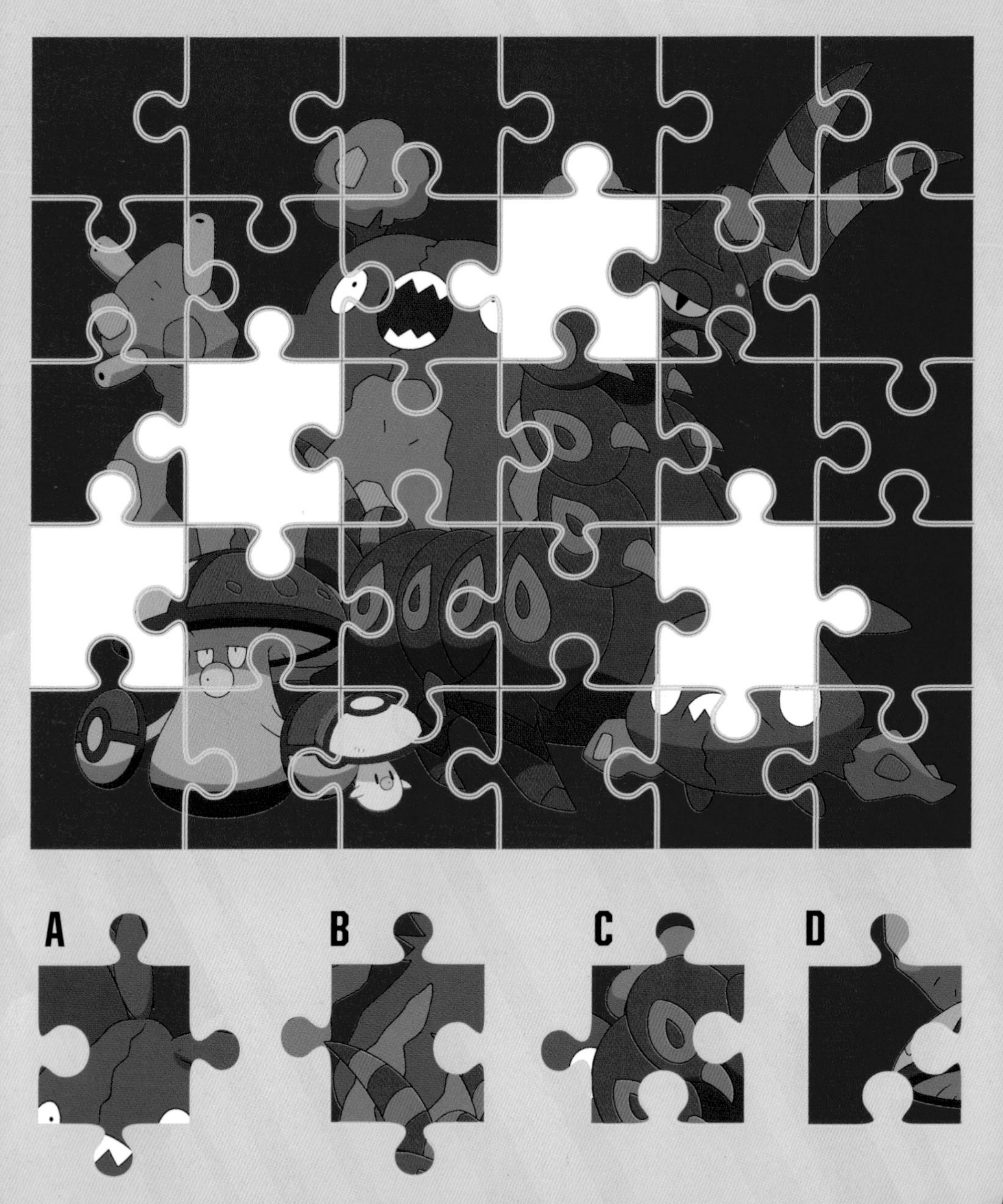

Turn to page 185 for the answers.

ODD POKÉMON OUT!

So you know your Pokémon by sight, but do you know them by type? Show your expertise and sort out the Pokémon that stand out in a crowd.

RULES: For this test, we're going to show you some different Pokémon. One of these Pokémon doesn't belong in the group, but which one? And what is the group? We'll give you three clues. You score yourself by how many clues you used!

CLUE #2:
Some are toxic

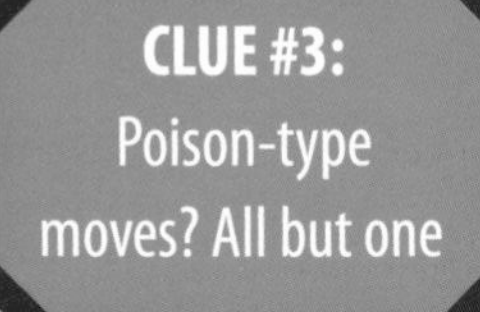

SCORE

1 clue: Wow! Maybe you should head up a team of your own!

2 clues: You're doing really well! You'll be a Trainer in no time!

3 clues: You'll be awesome on our Pokémon team!

Turn to page 185 for the answers.

POKÉMON SUDOKU

Trainers should keep themselves sharp, both in mind and body—
and Sudoku is a great way to keep your wits sharp! Use just the numbers 1–9.
Each number can appear only one time in a row, column, and box. Go to it, Trainers!

3	5	1		8			4	6
	9	7	6	5	4	1	8	
		4	3	7				9
1	2			4	9	3	6	7
	7	9	8		6	4	1	
4	3	6	2	1			9	5
9	1	5	7		8	6		
	6	3	4	9			7	1
	4	2	1	6	3	9	5	8

Turn to page 185 for the answers.

TYPE CAST!

Pokémon identification requires that a Trainer also know the type of Pokémon he or she is facing. This is extremely important when battling Pokémon, since type advantages could easily turn a battle! So see if you can match the Pokémon on the left to their types on the right.

POISON

BUG-POISON

GRASS-POISON

Turn to page 185 for the answers.

GROUND TYPES

STAY GROUNDED!

How well do you know your Ground types, Trainer? Let's see if you can answer a few questions about their habits, evolutions, and moves. If you can figure this out, you deserve a gold star!

ACROSS

3. Cilan has this dual-type Pokémon in his party.

5. What is the only Unova Pokémon that is a pure Ground type?

8. A Legendary Ground- and Flying-type Pokémon.

10. At Dan's resort, which Pokémon is responsible for the craters?

11. Excadrill is used by which Trainer?

12. Name one of the types that is most effective against Ground types.

13. Which dual Ground type belongs to a Trainer named Luke?

DOWN

1. Palpitoad evolves from which Pokémon?

2. What does the lead Sandile wear?

4. Name another type that is very effective against Ground types.

6. Complete this Evolution chain: Sandile, ______________, Krookodile.

7. What is the final type that is very effective against Ground types?

9. Name one of the types that Ground types are most effective against.

Turn to page 185 for the answers.

HAIKU

Oh, Ground-type Pokémon, how we love you so! You're steady and powerful, and you make us feel protected. Hmm, that makes a good start to a haiku! Wait—no it doesn't! It has far too many syllables! Compose one of your own to show how dedicated you are to your Ground-type Pokémon!

RULES: Haikus are composed of three lines, with five syllables in the first line, seven in the second line, and five in the last line. Try to match the syllable counts to compose a beautiful haiku for your Pokémon!

HAIKU

To ______________________
(Ground-type Pokémon)

The mighty ______________ ______________ .
(ground, land, rock) (swells, quakes, breaks)

______________ **fills enemies'** ______________ .
(terror, despair, horror) (hearts, minds, souls)

But you stand ______________ .
(bravely, strongly, sturdy)

WALL SCRAWL

Your adventure has given you some clues about Pokémon in your area! Other explorers have left messages about the Pokémon they've seen. Can you decipher these hastily worded scrawls?

Turn to page 186 for the answers.

EXCADRILL, WHERE ARE YOU?

Iris's Excadrill has a history of being, well, a bit of a difficult Pokémon. But Iris won't give up on it! She knows that Excadrill needs patience and practice to make it a great battle partner. But, Excadrill has used the move Dig and become lost underground! Help Excadrill find its way back to Iris!

Turn to page 186 for the answer.

FINISH THIS POKÉMON!

Well done! You've passed a tricky series of challenges to see if you really know your Pokémon! Now, we're setting a challenge to find out if you can remember what you've seen! Below is a Pokémon—color it in, and make sure you keep it neat and tidy! No Trainer wants a sloppy-looking Pokémon!

Turn to page 186 for the answer.

PIECE OF MINE

Your last visual test, Trainer! Can you tell which piece of the Pokémon is highlighted? Match the Pokémon pieces with the Pokémon to which they belong. Be careful! Some Ground types look suspiciously alike!

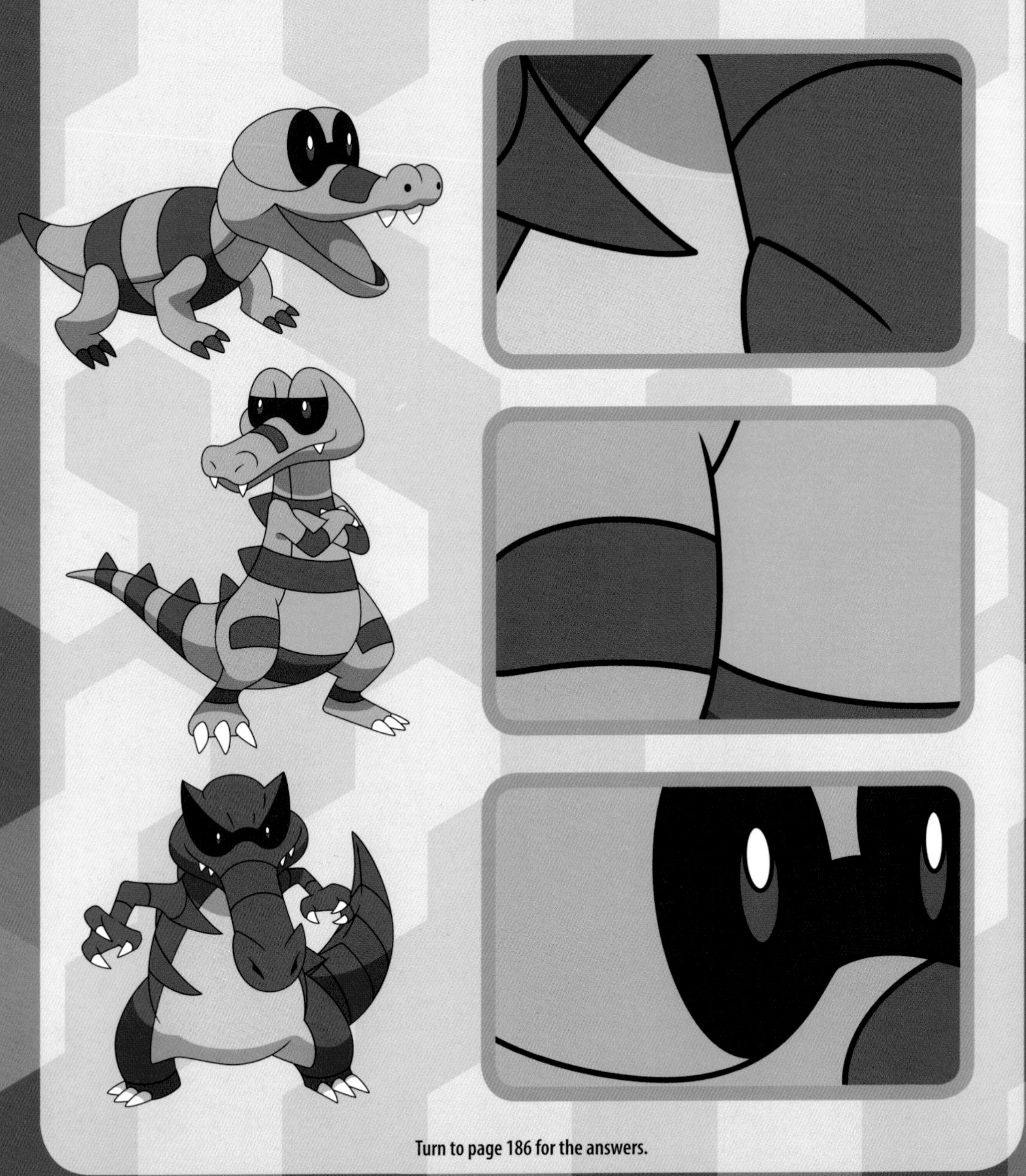

Turn to page 186 for the answers.

MATCH THE MOVE

Well, you stood your ground on that last one! Congratulations! Now, let's see how well you can match Ground-type Pokémon and their moves. Can you match the Pokémon on the left with their moves on the right? You've done it before with other types—can you do it again?

Turn to page 186 for the answers.

TRAINER PAGES

TRIP

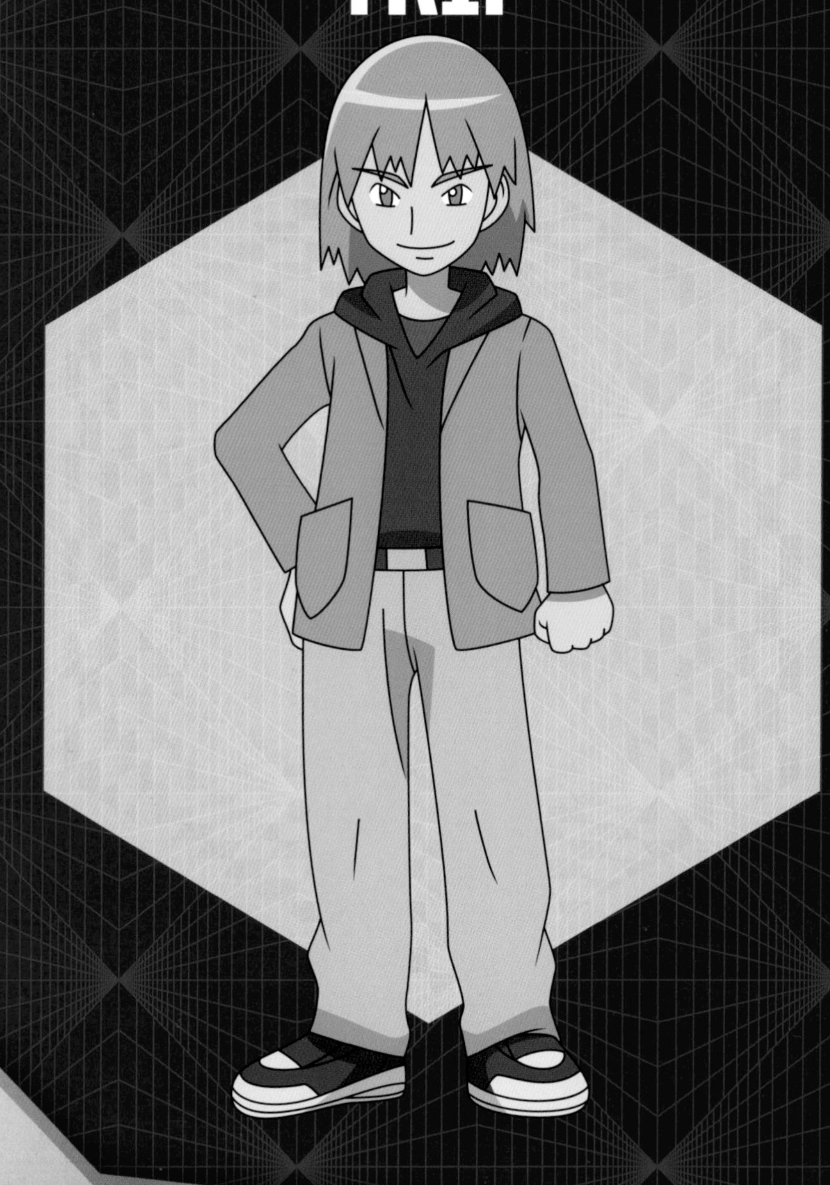

WHO'S YOUR FRIEND?

Knowing other Trainers in the Unova region is helpful, and you may even form bonds with others that will last a lifetime! Check your knowledge of other Trainers in Unova by correctly guessing which Pokémon travel with this Trainer!

Trip can be outspoken, brash, and a real know-it-all—but he also has raised and trained his Pokémon well. Identify which Pokémon Trip has (or has had) in his party from the lineup below!

Turn to page 186 for the answer.

TRAVEL CHECKLIST

Are you ready to go out in the world and make your mark as a Trainer? Make sure you have a travel checklist handy. Who would you visit during your journey to make sure your Pokémon were in tip-top shape?

PROFESSOR JUNIPER?

OFFICER JENNY?

NURSE JOY?

TEAM ROCKET?

Turn to page 186 for the answer.

DOTS WHAT I'M TALKING ABOUT!

A Pokémon Trainer doesn't catch Pokémon with one eye closed—not even the great Trainers can! They hone their sight to spot the shyest and most reclusive Pokémon. See if you can spot the Pokémon lurking in these dots. We'll even help out with some clues!

CLUE #1: Trip's first pick can eventually evolve into this. . .

CLUE #2: It is superior to most Grass types?

CLUE #3: The last Evolution of Snivy

SCORE

1 clue: Wow! Maybe you should head up a team of your own!

2 clues: You're doing really well! You'll be a Trainer in no time!

3 clues: You'll be awesome on our Pokémon team!

Turn to page 186 for the answer.

IS THAT WHAT YOU THINK IT IS?

Sometimes, your eyes can play tricks on you. Heat waves may cause your eyes to see a watery oasis where none exists. And no matter how hard you squint, that C you got in Science is never going to turn into an A! When traveling throughout Unova, you'll see lots of shapes in the high grass, watery puddles, and dim forests. But that doesn't mean you're seeing Pokémon—does it?

Are those shapes just playing tricks on your eyes, or are they actually Pokémon? See if you can match these silhouettes to the Pokémon they belong to! Draw a line from the outline to the Pokémon it looks like. Good luck!

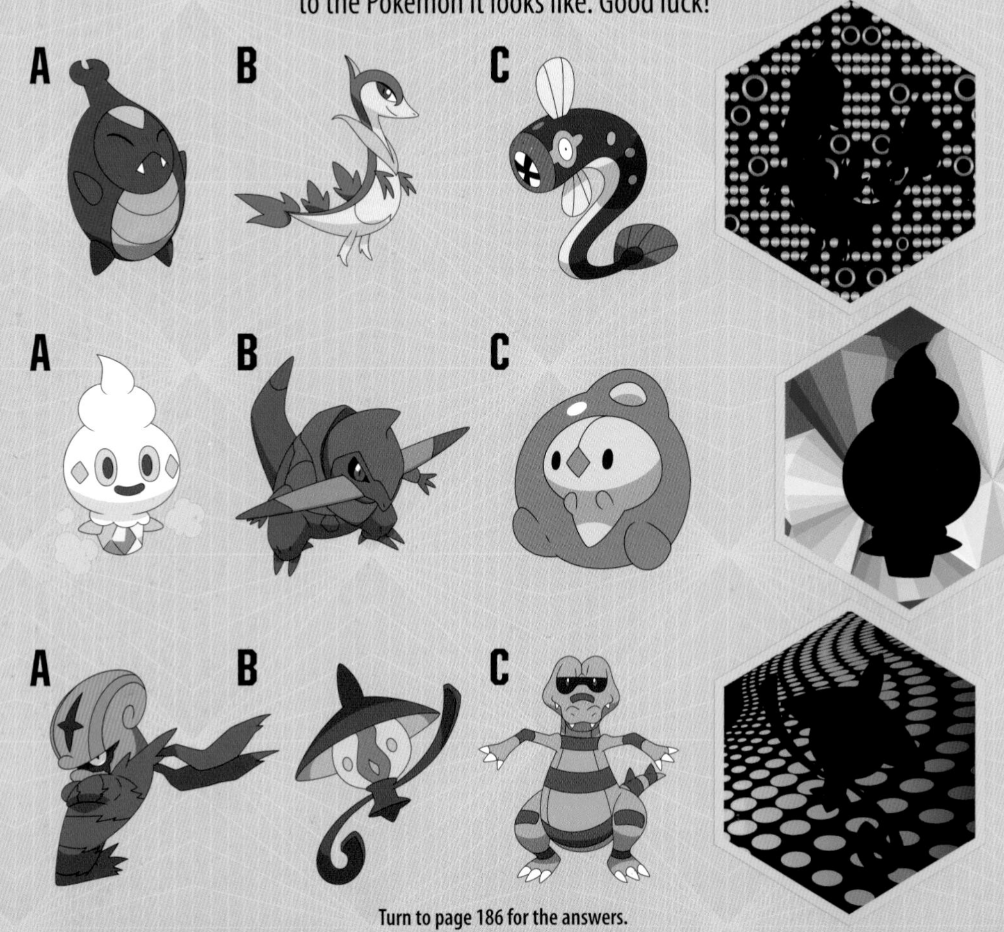

Turn to page 186 for the answers.

THE POKÉMON NAME GAME

Speed means a lot to a Trainer, and identifying your Pokémon and knowing their capabilities immediately is a key component of your training. Here's a one-, two-, or multi-player word game that tests how quick you are with your Pokémon.

RULES: You and a friend pick out a Unova Pokémon. Each of you then writes that Pokémon's name down on a piece of paper. Now, come up with as many words as you can from the letters in that Pokémon's name, within a two-minute time limit! The player with the most words wins!

EXAMPLE:

BONUS

Use the memory cards in the back of this book. Flip them face down, then pick one card and use the Pokémon on that card as your choice. If you pick a Fighting-type Pokémon, you score a five-point bonus!

CRYPTOGLYPHICS

Can you decipher the following coded message? Use the clues from the Pokémon that we've found out so far...

_ _ _ _ knows that sometimes

you just have to _ _ _ _ _ _

forward and _ _ _ _ _.

Strategy and _ _ _ _ _ are part of

a _ _ _ _ _ _ _'_ regimen,

but knowing your opponent's

weaknesses is also _ _ _ !

LEGEND

Turn to page 186 for the answers.

KNOWLEDGE BASE

It's time for another quiz, Trainer! To become a truly seasoned Trainer, you should start by answering all the following questions correctly. Can you?

1. Who does Trip select as his first Pokémon?

   ____

2. What type is this Pokémon?

   ____

3. How does he acquire this Pokémon?

   ____

4. What is the first move this Pokémon uses?

   ____

5. Who wins their first battle together, Ash or Trip?

   ____

6. Trip's primary Pokémon evolves into this Pokémon first...

   ____

7. What does Trip always carry with him?

   ____

8. What Ghost- and Fire-type Pokémon does Trip have?

   ____

9. Trip's Pidove evolved into this Pokémon.

   ____

10. What is another Pokémon on Trip's team?

    ____

Turn to page 186 for the answers.

WORD SCRAMBLE

Observing the behavior of a Pokémon and learning from that behavior can be daunting—Pokémon communication is still dicey at best. But a Good Trainer can take gibberish and turn it into something usable, if they know how to decipher certain clues, like the ones below!

RULES: Unscramble each word. In the letters that form that word, there is a secret letter that is surrounded by a box. Those letters will spell out the answer!

QUESTION

What is the goal of any worthy Pokémon Trainer?

1. The Fresh Snow Pokémon.

LIVANETIL _ _ _ _ _ _ _ _ ☐ _

2. An Axew Evolution.

SHUAXOR _ _ _ ☐ _ _ _

3. This Pokémon is ice-cold furry fury.

TRACEBI ☐ ☐ _ _ _ _ _

4. Ash's Pidove evolves into this when Trip's same Pokémon comes to its rescue.

QUAINTLRL ☐ _ _ _ _ _ _ _ _

5. Trip uses this Pokémon in his rematch with Ash.

LIFSRHLI _ _ _ _ _ _ _ ☐

6. Trip's Snivy evolves into this before Ash's does.

VESRENI _ ☐ _ _ _ _ _

7. Bianca's Pignite may evolve into this.

BEAROM _ _ ☐ _ _ _

8. The last Evolution of Timburr.

DRUCKREONL _ _ _ _ ☐ _ _ _ _ _

9. Cilan's Pokémon in the Striaton City Gym.

SPEANAG _ _ _ ☐ _ _ _

10. A loud little Pokémon that lives on the bottom of a lake.

EMPLOYT ☐ _ _ _ _ _ _

ANSWER

☐☐ ☐☐ ☐☐☐ ☐☐☐☐!

Turn to page 186 for the answers.

COMPLETING THE TRAINER HELPS COMPLETE YOUR TRAINING!

Great job on identifying the Pokémon types. You really are headed to the Pokémon Trainer Hall of Fame! Now let's meet a Trainer who is also Ash's rival—the sometimes condescending, arrogant, yet undoubtedly skilled Trainer named Trip! You may have seen Trip before, but can you remember what colors he wears? Finish this picture of Trip, making sure to get every detail just right. Trip hates sloppy Trainers!

Turn to page 186 for the answer.

POKÉMON ACROSTICS!

Let's play a game to help you get to know your Pokémon.
This is a fun game that can be played with one, two, or multiple players.

RULES: Pick a Pokémon name. Write that name in a column.
If you picked Servine, you should have a puzzle that looks like this:

Now, try to spell the longest word you can with the letters in each row. For example, starting with the first row, try to spell a word that starts with S, but is very long—like silhouette! You can only make one word per row, but you get one point for each letter used. Try for the longest words you know!

BONUS

Time the game—see how many words you can come up with in two minutes!

BONUS

Use the memory cards in the back of this book. Flip them face down, then pick one card and use the Pokémon on that card as your choice. If you pick an Electric-type Pokémon, you score a five-point bonus!

Pokémon Super Activity Book: Do You Know Unova?

Certificate of Completion

This is to show that

____

is a

Issued this ______

day of______________________,

20_____.

ICE TYPES

WORD SEARCH—ICE!

You're coming down the final stretch, Trainer! These last four types may prove to be the hardest yet. But we know you can do it! Now, to find Ice-type Pokémon, you have to travel far and search wide! We're sure you know what you're looking for, though—pick out only the Ice types (or dual types with Ice being one of the types) from the puzzle below.

J K C V E P V K I T R E Z J N B S A M U R O T T R
Q Z R L L F F V L W V K W D B G M L S C L O I O E
R B N Z P N A I F L U H M K N O Z M S U I E I E M
V E G L Q S S C F J O V A N I L L I S H U R N E B
V A J K A W I V Q D D S D A H I Y Y K K E X X D O
A R W G A A R C H E O P S E I I A L J P G U B Z A
E T F Y U L V A N I L L I T E Q F F R Y L M Y L R
Z I P B G O L U R K N X E O G F M E H L V Q A O T
B C S L D F K P Q C M L N U P Z S Y I J O N Y C Z
Y Q B G A R B A D O R B I Y B M X N E U O H N Z Q
P Y P J V Y W K M H W C P G U Z A J M G G K D G Z
G C U B C H O O W F R A E D C V K C O F L Z X U M
S H Q G I Q X U N F E Z A N T X K Y Q O N D O X O
S U Y Q F W Z F G W T A Y M P S R X B H F A D H R
D P C Q F I Z D W Q P E T Z P C F L P T O U K J T

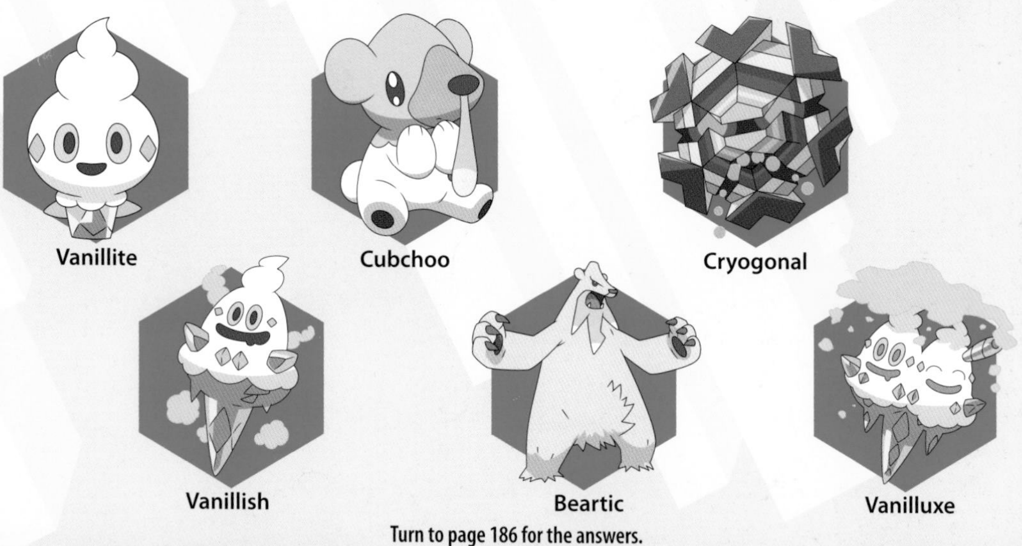

Turn to page 186 for the answers.

POKÉMON FINDER

Okay, enough with the easy stuff. Now find ten Ice-type Pokémon among these ice floes. Remember, close your eyes, trust your instincts, and chip away at these frosty floes!

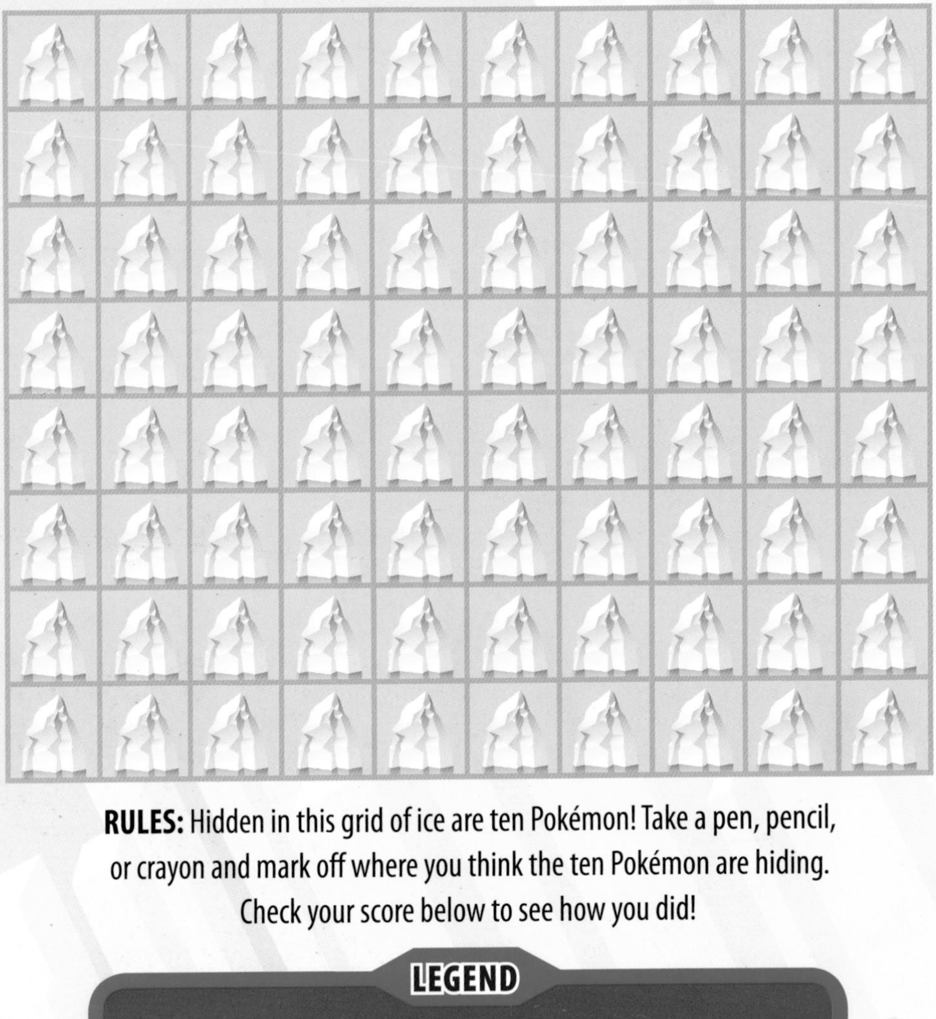

RULES: Hidden in this grid of ice are ten Pokémon! Take a pen, pencil, or crayon and mark off where you think the ten Pokémon are hiding. Check your score below to see how you did!

LEGEND

0–3 catches: You'll be awesome on our Pokémon team!
4–7 catches: You're doing really well! You'll be a Trainer in no time!
7–10 catches: Wow! Maybe you should head up a team of your own!

Turn to page 186 for the answers.

FIND THE DIFFERENCE

Nice throwing arm you've got there, Trainer. You should consider using that strength to help train your Pokémon for some really serious challenges! But before we get ahead of ourselves, try once again to see if you can spot which one of these Ice-type Pokémon is an imposter!

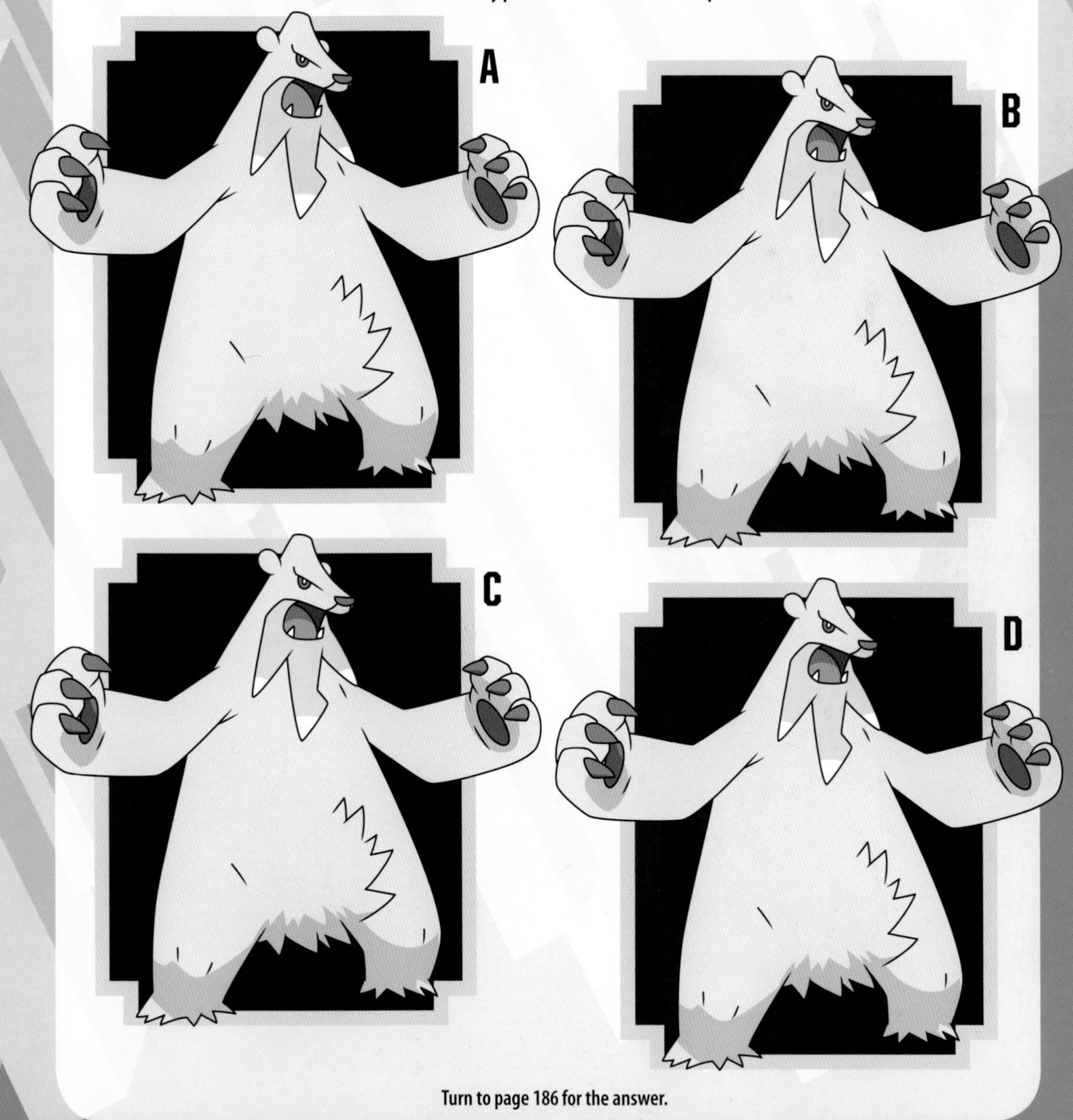

Turn to page 186 for the answer.

MATCH THE MOVE

Good job! You can give your eyes a rest, because we're going to work on your brain instead. Remember your training—certain Pokémon are known for their signature moves. Can you match the Pokémon on the left with their moves on the right?

Turn to page 186 for the answers.

POKÉMON SEEK AND FIND

Be advised that four Ice-type Pokémon were seen traveling with a large group of Pokémon. Identify the four Ice types in the following picture, and then report back to us. That is all.

Turn to page 187 for the answers.

DARK TYPES

EVOLUTION REVOLUTION!

So mysterious, so unknown—Dark types have characteristics all their own! Dark-type Pokémon can be powerful allies, as well as fearsome opponents. Can you fill in the missing Evolutions of these Dark-type Pokémon?

Turn to page 187 for the answers.

A PUZZLE OF POKÉMON

Let's see how well you can assemble the information at hand to help identify Pokémon—draw a line from each puzzle piece to where it should go in the puzzle!

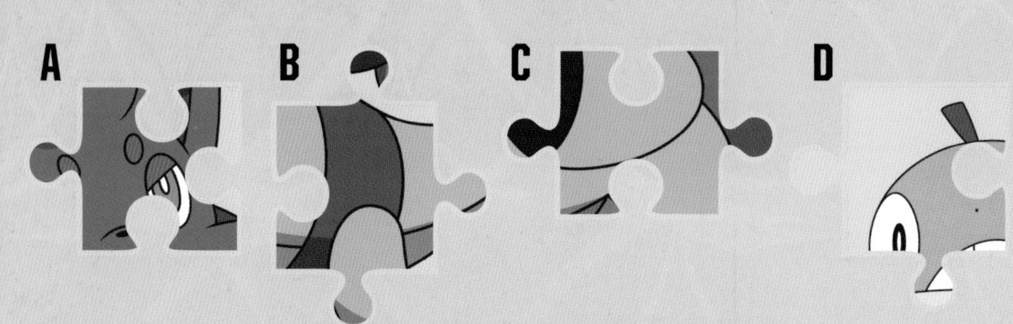

Turn to page 187 for the answers.

ODD POKÉMON OUT!

So many Pokémon, so many ways to catalogue them! The Pokédex does a great job, but what happens when you're away from your equipment? Can you classify Pokémon using sight alone?

RULES: In this test, you'll see some different Pokémon. One of these Pokémon doesn't belong in the group, but which one? And what is the group? We'll give you three clues. You score yourself by how many clues you used!

CLUE #1: All of them are Dark types.

CLUE #2: Some of them are not evolving anymore.

CLUE #3: One has another step to go.

SCORE

1 clue: Wow! Maybe you should head up a team of your own!

2 clues: You're doing really well! You'll be a Trainer in no time!

3 clues: You'll be awesome on our Pokémon team!

Turn to page 187 for the answers.

POKÉMON SUDOKU

Trainers should keep themselves sharp, both in mind and body—and Sudoku is a great way to keep your wits sharp! Use just the numbers 1–9. Each number can appear only one time in a row, column, and box. Go to it, Trainers!

2		1		6			7	
	7			4			6	
9		4		5		3	1	
7		9	6	2	8		3	
6		8				9	2	7
5		2	1	7	9		8	
	2		3	8	5			6
1		5		9			4	3
	9			1		8	5	2

Turn to page 187 for the answers.

TYPE CAST!

When battling, knowing the type of Pokémon you're facing is hugely important—it can mean the difference between winning or losing the battle. When you know what you're facing, you can make sure to send the right type of Pokémon out! See if you can match the Pokémon on the left with its types on the right.

DARK-DRAGON

DARK-FIGHTING

DARK-FLYING

Turn to page 187 for the answers.

NORMAL TYPES

EVERYTHING'S BACK TO NORMAL!

Normal type Pokémon can fool you—they don't seem so tough, and then just when you think the tide of battle is turning in your favor. . . BAM! You're knocked sideways! See what you remember about Normal types by answering the tough questions in this crossword puzzle.

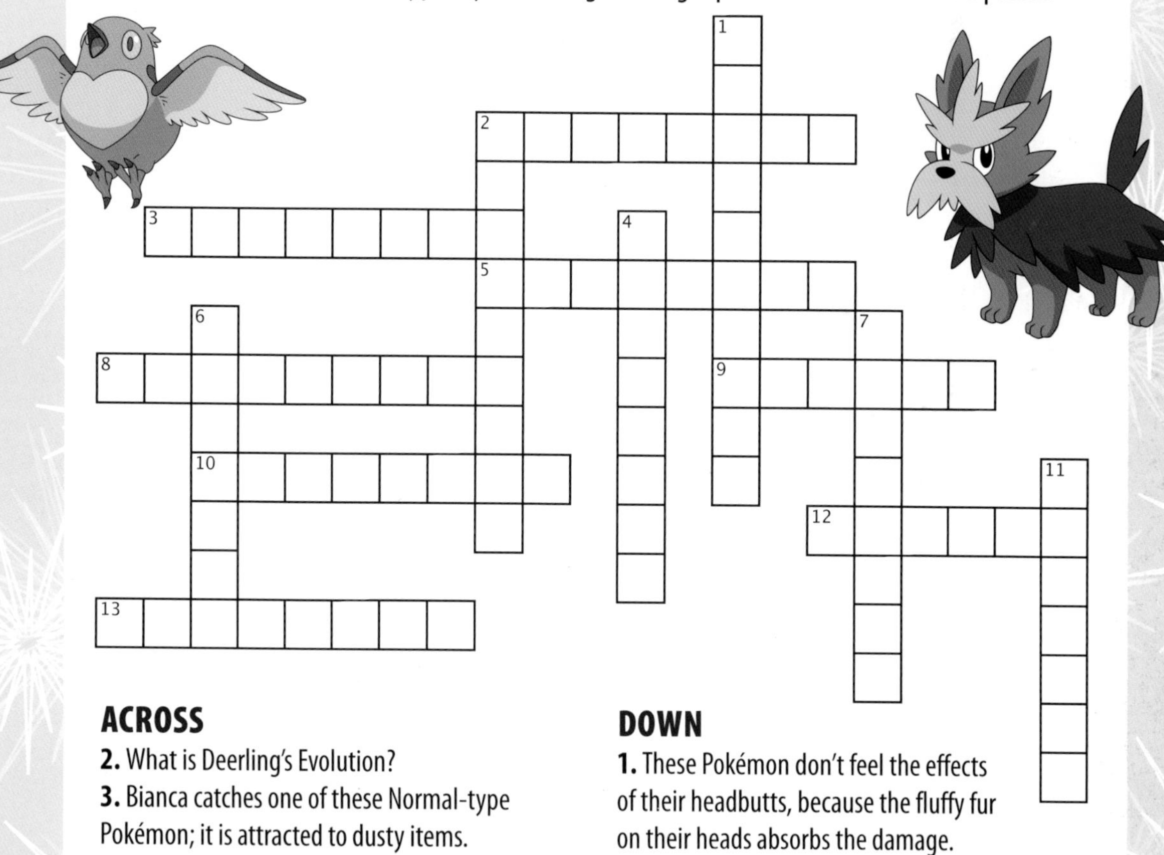

ACROSS

2. What is Deerling's Evolution?

3. Bianca catches one of these Normal-type Pokémon; it is attracted to dusty items.

5. What is the last Evolution of Pidove?

8. When he has his rematch with Ash, Trip calls on the Evolution of the Pokémon Ash first caught in Unova. What is it?

9. This Pokémon is always at Nurse Joy's side.

10. This is the Evolution of Minccino.

12. This is the first Pokémon Ash caught in Unova. It happens to be a Normal and Flying type!

13. Normal types are weak against this type!

DOWN

1. These Pokémon don't feel the effects of their headbutts, because the fluffy fur on their heads absorbs the damage.

2. What is the last Evolution of Lillipup?

4. Ash sees herds of these Normal- and Grass-type Pokémon. Their coloring changes with the seasons.

6. This is one of the Normal types Lenora used in her Gym battle against Ash.

7. Iris thinks this Pokémon is so cute—everyone loves the Puppy Pokémon!

11. By the time Lenora had her rematch with Ash, one of her Pokémon evolved into this.

Turn to page 187 for the answers.

HAIKU

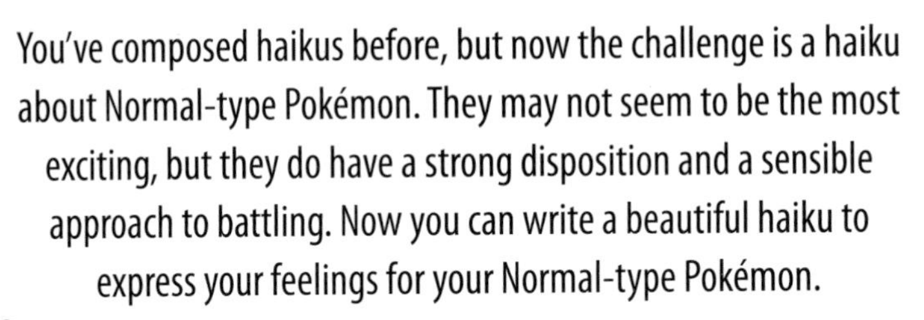

You've composed haikus before, but now the challenge is a haiku about Normal-type Pokémon. They may not seem to be the most exciting, but they do have a strong disposition and a sensible approach to battling. Now you can write a beautiful haiku to express your feelings for your Normal-type Pokémon.

RULES: Haikus are composed of three lines, with five syllables in the first line, seven in the second line, and five in the last line. Try to match the syllable counts as you compose a beautiful haiku for your Pokémon!

HAIKU

To ______________________________
(Normal-type Pokémon)

You can ______________________ **any that**
(fight, stand, brave)

come our way, but we can ________________
(love, hold, hug)

you ____________________ **in our** ________________.
(happily, forever, cheerfully,) (arms, hearts, minds)

WALL SCRAWL

Your adventure has led you to some clues about Pokémon in your area! Other explorers have left you messages about the Pokémon they've seen. Can you decipher these hastily worded scrawls?

Turn to page 187 for the answers.

PATRAT STAMPEDE!

A group of Patrat are stampeding and thundering across the hills near Nuvema Town! But, in their haste, they have left one of their own behind. Help that lone Patrat get back to the herd!

Turn to page 187 for the answer.

FINISH THIS POKÉMON!

Can you remember what the different colors of a Pokémon look like? You're a Trainer, so you should be able to correctly color this Pokémon using only your memory. You should have no trouble at all, right? Good luck! See if you know your Pokémon as well as you think you do!

Turn to page 187 for the answer.

POKÉMON FUN TIME!

WHAT'S IN THE POKÉ BALL?

Someone was sure in a hurry—they left a Poké Ball behind, with some notes about the Pokémon inside. You should drop it off at the nearest Pokémon Center, but first try to find out what's in the Poké Ball. See if you can guess which Pokémon is in the Poké Ball just by the clues!

See how fast you can figure out what's in the Poké Ball! Score is based on how many clues you use!

CLUE #1: Bug type

CLUE #2: But wait! Also a Grass type!

CLUE #3: The Nurturing Pokémon

CLUE #4: One belonged to Luke

CLUE #5: Ash once battled one of these

CLUE #6: Costume maker

CLUE #7: Skilled at sewing

CLUE #8: Guardian of Burgh's Gym

CLUE #9: Starts with an "L"

CLUE #10: One of the evolved forms of Sewaddle

SCORING

1–3 clues: Wow! Maybe you should head up a team of your own!

4–7 clues: You're doing really well! You'll be a Trainer in no time!

8–10 clues: You'll be awesome on our Pokémon team!

Turn to page 187 for the answer.

POKÉ BALL MATCHUP

Okay, one more lesson on Poké Balls. Every good Trainer needs to know their Poké Ball functions, and this exercise will help you. Match the Poké Ball with the Pokémon that it would be most effective at catching.

ULTRA BALL
Has a very good success rate when capturing Pokémon in the wild.

PIDOVE
A wild Pidove that you add to your team, even though you have one already!

TIMER BALL
Works best after battling a Pokémon for a long time.

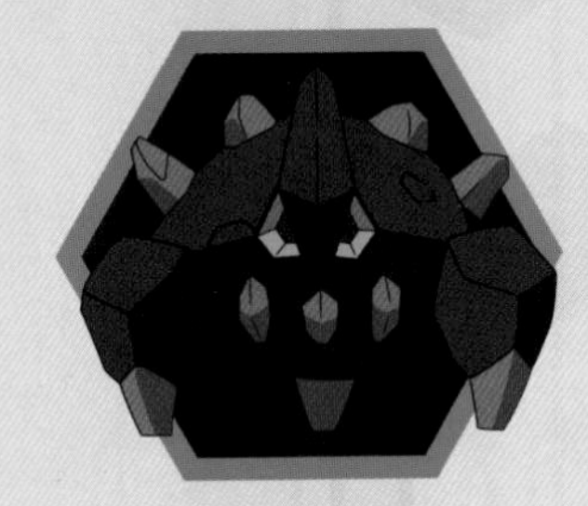

BOLDORE
A Boldore that you've been battling for a while!

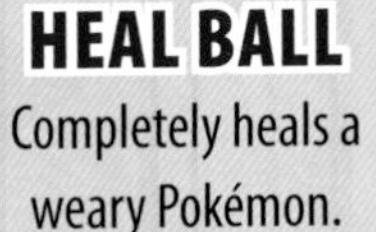

HEAL BALL
Completely heals a weary Pokémon.

LEAVANNY
A Leavanny that has almost fainted, but that you want to use in your next battle!

REPEAT BALL
Works better on Pokémon you've caught before.

SWANNA
A Swanna you've weakened but could not catch with a standard Poké Ball!

Turn to page 187 for the answers.

WHAT KIND OF TRAINER ARE YOU?

Are you the kind of Trainer that runs from every wild Pokémon you see? Or are you the kind of Trainer that gives it everything you've got?

You are battling a Galvantula.

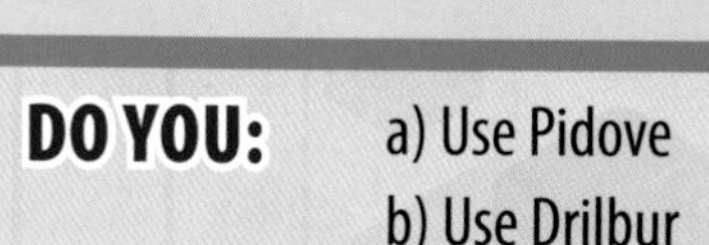

a) Use Pidove
b) Use Drilbur
c) Use Joltik

You have a strong Water-type Pokémon in Samurott, and it has been defeating the opposing Pokémon in a three-on-three battle. But now you have to make a choice—against what seems to be an equally tough Alomomola.

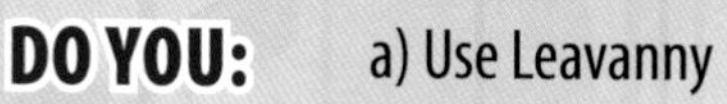

a) Use Leavanny
b) Use Samurott
c) Use Emboar

You're facing Beartic, an Ice-type Pokémon that has the advantage over Dragon types.

a) Use Axew
b) Use Heatmor
c) Use Serperior

Turn to page 187 for the answers.

SAY WHAT?

The following has been heard around Unova.
Can you identify who said it?

"I'm sure science has the key! Scientific perspective is what we need!"

"When it comes to Pokémon in the Unova region, there's so much stuff I don't know..."

"I'm afraid Excadrill's acting a bit chilly..."

"I couldn't care less about your reasons! The end result is what counts!"

"Your battle style has no spice and your attacks are rather bland."

"I know the forest's voice when I hear it!"

"That's basic."

"Hey, I just caught a Sewaddle! Isn't that cool, Professor?"

Turn to page 187 for the answers.

WHO AM I?

You'll meet lots of people on your journey—and you'll find it takes skill and patience to remember everyone's name! There are key people you simply cannot ignore, people vital to your adventure. See if you can identify who these people are!

CLUE #1: She's part of a legacy.
CLUE #2: Don't mess with her.
CLUE #3: Spends a lot of time handling Team Rocket.
CLUE #4: Has a whole force behind her.
CLUE #5: Never misses a beat.
CLUE #6: Uniform-ity.
CLUE #7: Never gives up.
CLUE #8: Helps at the Dreamyard.
CLUE #9: Guards the Skyarrow Bridge.
CLUE #10: She's the law.

CLUE #1: Brainy.
CLUE #2: Lives in Nuvema Town.
CLUE #3: Respected.
CLUE #4: Friends with Oak.
CLUE #5: She gives you choices.
CLUE #6: Tech wizard.
CLUE #7: She has a Pokédex for everyone.
CLUE #8: Lab work doesn't bother her.
CLUE #9: Always on that Xtransceiver.
CLUE #10: Unova's professor.

SCORE
1–3 clues: Wow! Maybe you should head up a team of your own!
4–7 clues: You're doing really well! You'll be a Trainer in no time!
8–10 clues: You'll be awesome on our Pokémon team!

Turn to page 187 for the answers.

SHOW YOUR COLORS!

Get creative and show your Pokémon how proud of them you are. Create your own Pokémon flag to wave whenever you see your Pokémon!

STEP ONE: Draw your favorite Pokémon

STEP TWO: Add symbols that represent your Pokémon (Fire type, Water type, Grass type, etc.)

STEP THREE: Color your flag in with any colors that you think represent your Pokémon!

BATTLE PLAN

All right Trainers! Time for some battle situations that require a little thought and a lot of strategy! Let's see how you face off against the team below. Choose which of your three Pokémon to use, and see how they do against these three Pokémon!

Ash has shown that type matchups don't always determine the winner—but they can still give you a real advantage in battle! If you need some tips for victory, try page 188!

YOUR TEAM:

BEARTIC

Moves

a) Icicle Crash

b) Slash

c) Blizzard

EMOLGA

Moves

a) Quick Attack

b) Discharge

c) Acrobatics

PALPITOAD

Moves

a) Supersonic

b) Mud Shot

c) Hydro Pump

YOUR OPPONENT'S TEAM:

LITWICK

Moves

a) Fire Spin

b) Shadow Ball

c) Astonish

FRILLISH

Moves

a) Absorb

b) Water Pulse

c) Night Shade

LEAVANNY

Moves

a) String Shot

b) Leaf Storm

c) X-Scissor

LIGHTS! CAMERA! POKÉMON!

Ever dream of making your very own Pokémon movie? Now you can, with this Pokémon Movie Maker! Simply add in the names of the characters you'd like to see, the Pokémon you'd like to direct, and the towns and situations you'd like to experience. Have Leavanny and Swadloon help you with the costumes, and have Zorua assist with the parts. Now help your team put this film together the right way!

MY POKÉMON MOVIE TITLE:________________________________

The Pokémon I would like to see in my movie:

1. ____________________

2. ____________________

3. ____________________

4. ____________________

5. ____________________

6. ____________________

7. ____________________

8. ____________________

The Trainers I would like to see:

1. ____________________

2. ____________________

3. ____________________

4. ____________________

The places I would visit:

1. ____________________

2. ____________________

3. ____________________

4. ____________________

The situation I would resolve:

1. There is a great, huge Pokémon bothering my village!

2. Some of the Pokémon are acting strange!

3. I think the forest ahead may be haunted!

WHODUNIT?

Some Pokémon have been spotted in areas nearby, and you have to decipher the clues they've left behind so you can track them down. How well do you know the tell-tale signs of a Pokémon? This whodunit will help hone your skills.

WHODUNIT?

The cold doesn't bother you, but tracking down this elusive Pokémon has been a chore. The cold wind blowing snow out of an ice cave makes you suspect your Pokémon is an Ice type. The frozen walls of the cave reveal huge slashes in the ice, marks that must have been made by an incredibly large Pokémon. Strands of white fur litter the back of a den. It can only be a ____________________!

WHODUNIT?

The dappled sunlight through the forest trees plays tricks on your eyes. You could have sworn you saw a bush full of leaves shake and fly right past you in the clearing ahead of you. Large green leaves are scattered everywhere, as are clothes sewn from the leaves. Sewaddle are crooning in the leaves above you, while Swadloon look expectantly toward the sunlight for the leader of this glade, a Pokémon that has evolved past them all.
Is it a ____________________?

WHODUNIT?

Oh, the smell! Rotting garbage and an undercurrent of food, trash, and sewage! How can any Pokémon make a home here? But one has, a Pokémon so deep in its own stench that it has become toxic to others. It's a Poison type that uses the garbage around it to channel energy into its battles. All it needs now is to find a few friends—and that kindergarten class looks like a good start! It can only be a
____________________!

Turn to page 188 for the answers.

BUG TYPES

EVOLUTION REVOLUTION!

Don't let the fact that they seem icky fool you—these Bug types are strong, dependable, and aggressive! Using them in your party will help you against the more defensive Pokémon that you meet. Let's see if you can identify the Evolution chain of the Bug-type Pokémon listed below!

Turn to page 188 for the answers.

A PUZZLE OF POKÉMON

Let's see how well you can assemble the information at hand to help identify Pokémon—draw a line from each puzzle piece to where it should go in the puzzle!

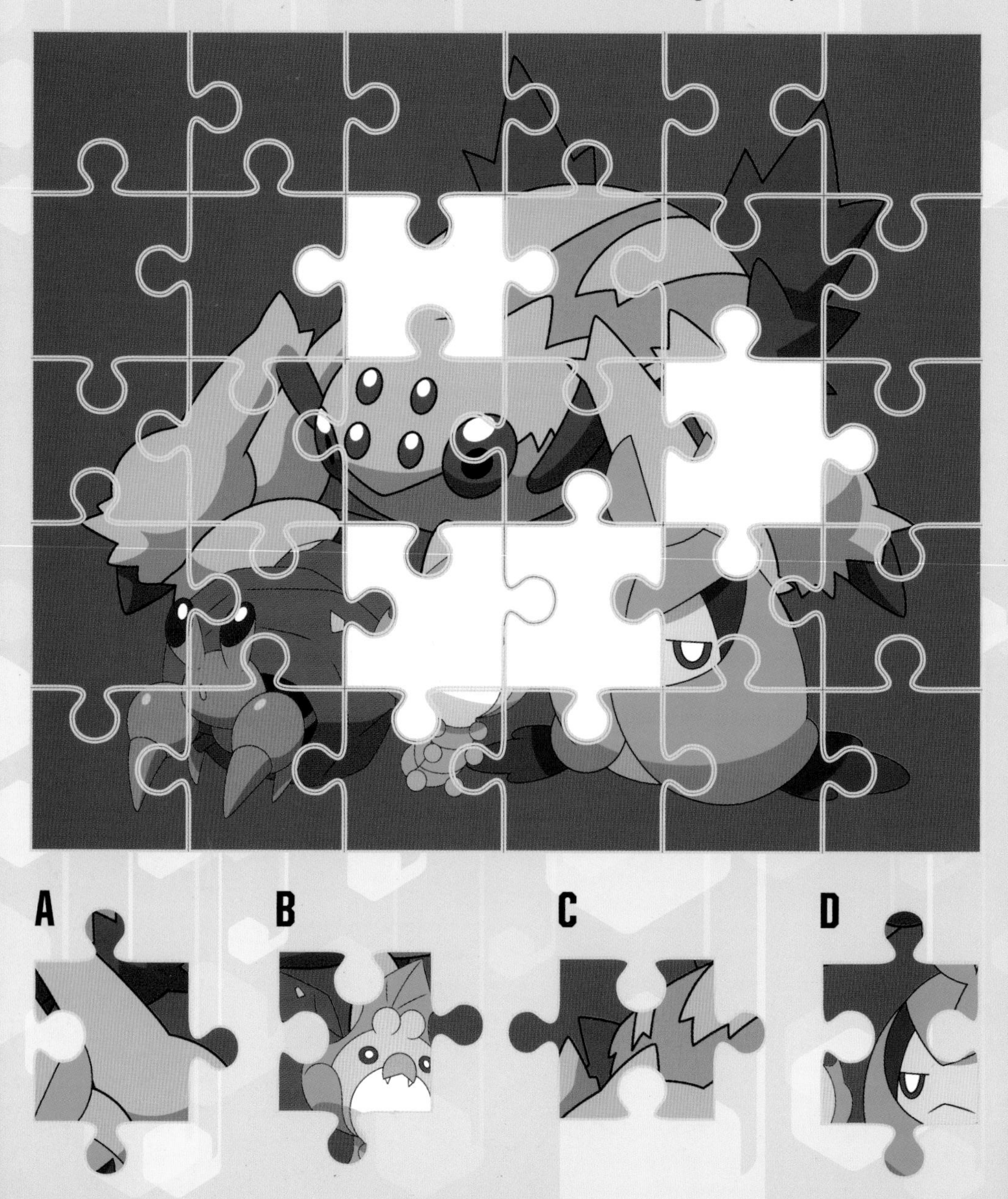

Turn to page 188 for the answers.

ODD POKÉMON OUT!

Let's put a group of Pokémon on the page, and see if you can tell why one of these does not belong with the others. We'll even throw in some clues, but we know you don't need them. Which one of these Pokémon does not belong here?

RULES: For this test, we're going to show you some different Pokémon. One of these Pokémon doesn't belong in the group, but which one? And what is the group? We'll give you three clues. You score yourself by how many clues you used!

CLUE #1: All of them are dual types.

CLUE #2: All of them are Steel types.

CLUE #3: Only one is not a Bug type.

SCORE

1 clue: Wow! Maybe you should head up a team of your own!
2 clues: You're doing really well! You'll be a Trainer in no time!
3 clues: You'll be awesome on our Pokémon team!

Turn to page 188 for the answers.

POKÉMON SUDOKU

Trainers should keep themselves sharp, both in mind and body—and Sudoku is a great way to keep your wits sharp! Use just the numbers 1–9. Each number can appear only one time in a row, column, and box. Go to it, Trainers!

				3	2			
	4	3		7	8		9	5
	2	7					6	3
4			7	2	5	3		
5					6		1	
8	7	9			3			2
		4	3	6	1	9		
	1			9			7	
2			8			4	3	1

Turn to page 188 for the answers.

TYPE CAST!

This is your last challenge! Good luck! Pokémon identification requires that a Trainer also know the type of Pokémon he or she is facing. This is extremely important when battling Pokémon, since type advantages can easily turn a battle! So, see if you can match the Pokémon on the left with their types on the right.

BUG-STEEL

BUG-POISON

BUG-ELECTRIC

Turn to page 188 for the answers.

ROCK TYPES

WORD SEARCH—ROCK!

Almost there, Trainer. Stay on target! Now that we've "bugged" you enough, we're ready to rock your world! In the word search below, look for the Rock types, or dual Rock types, and leave everyone else in the dust!

N	X	P	A	V	B	B	E	S	C	G	O	R	O	G	G	E	N	R	O	L	A	Q	P	Y
M	R	D	J	Z	N	Z	D	L	Q	U	S	E	R	P	E	R	I	O	R	L	J	F	C	T
O	S	Q	S	S	M	G	Z	K	W	F	C	C	H	M	B	O	Q	N	U	D	C	P	T	C
L	S	Z	W	W	A	U	B	O	R	S	F	E	U	Q	P	L	P	R	Q	X	J	E	J	R
R	U	S	Y	N	S	W	A	R	P	O	L	D	J	M	H	E	G	D	A	N	L	C	H	N
R	Y	C	O	X	W	R	S	O	P	T	O	T	N	F	H	M	S	K	C	O	F	A	A	S
O	E	F	P	R	C	A	E	B	S	R	M	K	U	S	P	B	X	E	G	K	S	R	G	R
K	V	M	P	N	G	H	T	U	U	C	V	R	O	Y	A	O	Y	Q	B	D	S	R	F	W
T	W	V	X	S	C	I	R	C	T	C	O	U	V	D	Y	A	I	N	O	W	U	A	O	B
H	S	A	X	R	L	C	G	I	H	H	K	L	G	L	I	R	M	K	L	E	W	C	M	A
W	Z	V	A	V	B	D	T	A	G	O	F	P	I	D	Z	L	C	V	D	B	P	O	R	W
H	A	R	C	H	E	N	Y	G	L	U	G	P	K	P	T	I	E	M	O	B	P	S	T	F
R	S	A	M	U	R	O	T	T	Z	I	T	N	A	P	E	K	A	H	R	L	C	T	B	Q
L	G	S	T	O	U	T	L	A	N	D	T	B	O	A	Q	D	S	E	E	E	C	A	E	K
U	V	T	E	T	I	R	T	O	U	G	A	H	K	N	N	Q	E	S	T	G	D	H	P	H

Turn to page 188 for the answers.

POKÉMON SEEK AND FIND

Either these Pokémon are getting easier to find, or you're getting better at spotting them! Look for six—that's right, six—Rock-type Pokémon hiding out in this pack!

Turn to page 188 for the answers.

POKÉMON FINDER

Okay, you're good at spotting Pokémon—
—now let's see how your throwing arm works!

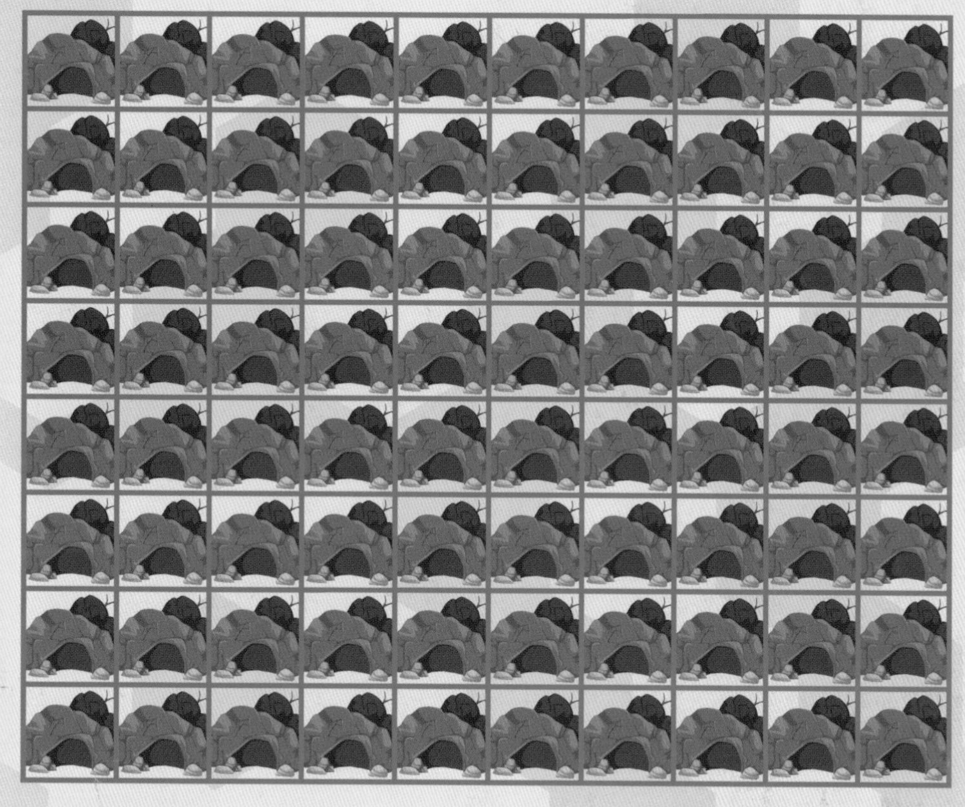

Hidden in this grid of deep, rocky caves are ten Pokémon! Take a pen, pencil, or crayon and mark off where you think the ten Pokémon are hiding. Check your score below to see how you did!

LEGEND

0–3 catches: You'll be awesome on our Pokémon team!
4–7 catches: You're doing really well! You'll be a Trainer in no time!
7–10 catches: Wow! Maybe you should head up a team of your own!

Turn to page 188 for the answers.

FIND THE DIFFERENCE

Wow, your Rock-type knowledge is as solid as a. . . oh, well, as solid as a rock! Good for you! Now it's time for a bit of a change-up! Can you spot which one of these Pokémon is an imposter? A false Pokémon is like a bit of glass among diamonds—weed it out and throw it away! Make sure to check colors, appendages, expressions—anything that can make a difference! Good luck!

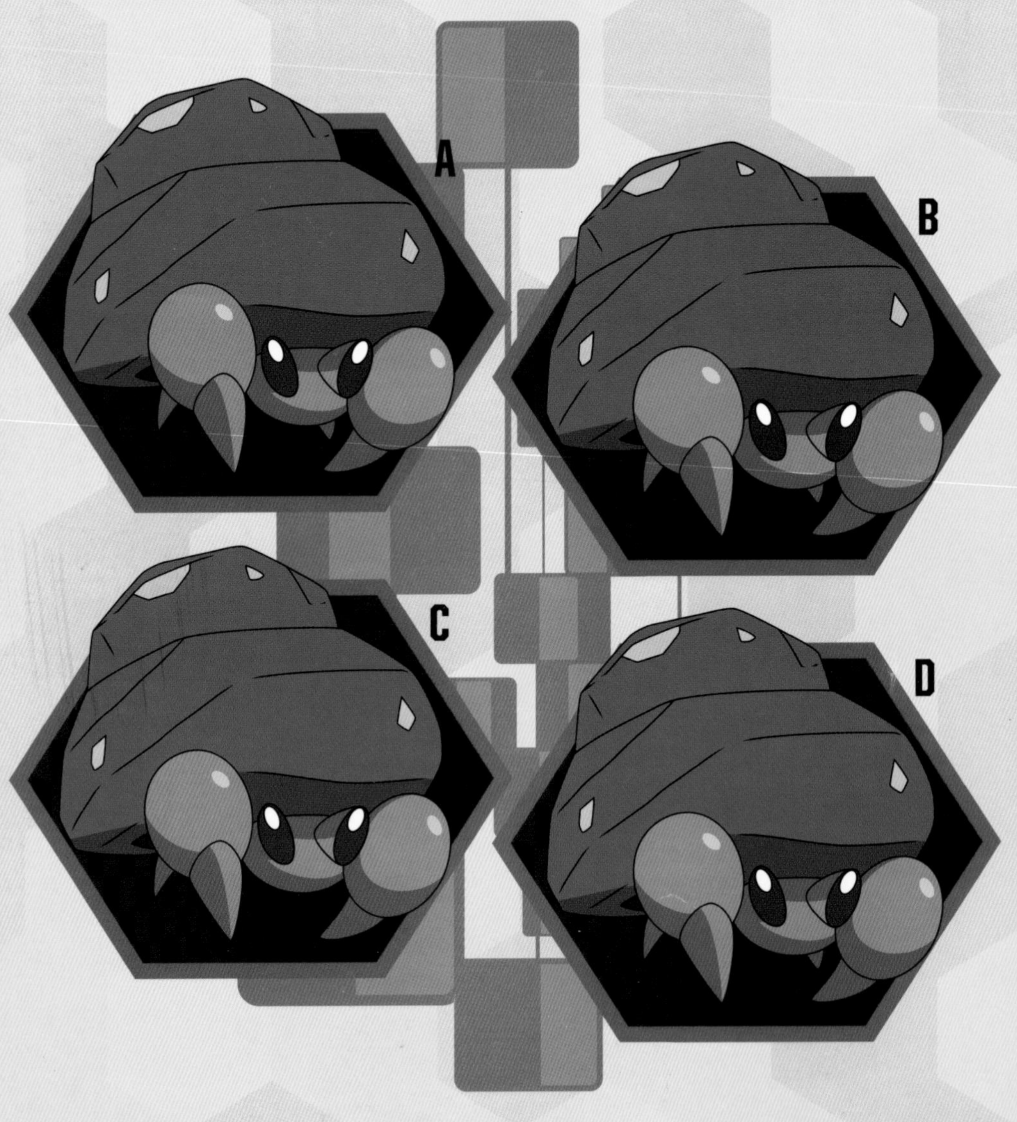

Turn to page 188 for the answer.

STOP, ROCK, AND ROLL!

Roggenrola has rolled down a small hill, and fallen into a deep, dark cave. Can you help this sturdy and dependable Rock type find its way back to its friends?

Turn to page 188 for the answer.

Pokémon Super Activity Book: Do You Know Unova?
Certificate of
Completion
This is to show that
__________________ is a
Ice-type
Pokémon Specialist
Dark-type
Pokémon Specialist
Rock-type
Pokémon Specialist
Normal-type
Pokémon Specialist
Bug-type
Pokémon Specialist
Issued this ______
day of______________,
20_____.

ANSWERS

Hold on—Trainers don't cheat! So, you'd better not sneak a peek back here unless you're ready to check your answers.

PAGE 7: WORD SEARCH —FIRE!

C X J S G L E Q E E O L N N B H B W L V R G K L V
H Z B U I T P A F P T R F L I T W I C K S W E T O
A B M V W M E B I X J L E M X S C P C J I X G V L
N K B S F G I K B E G J P A N S E A R Z J T Y U C
D R T A T N E S O C Z H I B H J Y F D E N T G I A
E W W R W H N Y E O Y H G H Y D N E R E M P K N R
L F L F K U E V O A A D N O D A M M P X L B K Z O
U R J J H B S A Y H R G I V H Q Q M O V O F O E N
R Q N T D E K V M X L B T A H T A S E E I R R A A
E R J Z E A A V F W M M E C M L A R V E S T A H R
K V I H M P H T Z N M Z B L P F C A M W Y Y U B G
S B I U U L I C M O B O W V V W H S C Q A S L I I
R J R Z P X H G A O M K D K S F M X M D A Y O G C
H A D O M I F G X H R Q V A J M Y K Y R H D Z O K
D A R M A N I T A N R H F Z L N X D R Y F C D P R

PAGE 8: POKÉMON FINDER

PAGE 9: FIND THE DIFFERENCE

D - missing thumb

PAGE 10: MATCH THE MOVE

HEATMOR – BUG BITE
LAMPENT – HEX
DARMANITAN – FIRE PUNCH

PAGE 11: POKÉMON SEEK AND FIND

PAGE 13: EVOLUTION REVOLUTION

C

PAGE 14: A PUZZLE OF POKÉMON

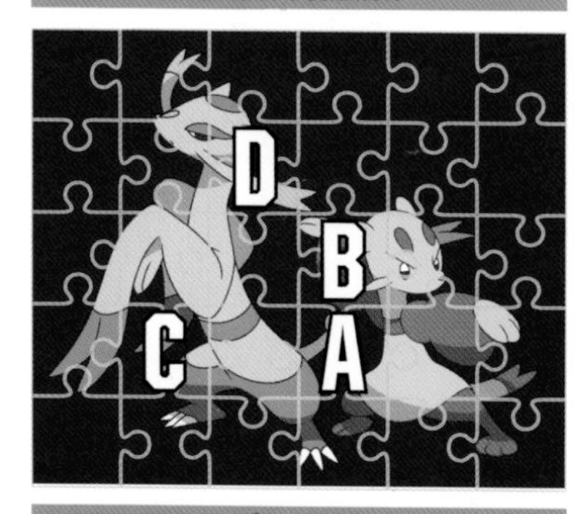

PAGE 15: ODD POKÉMON OUT!

SCRAGGY
Scraggy is the only Pokémon here that has not evolved!

PAGE 16: POKÉMON SUDOKU

4	7	6	2	5	9	8	3	1
2	5	1	6	3	8	4	7	9
8	9	3	7	4	1	5	2	6
5	6	4	9	2	3	7	1	8
9	3	2	1	8	7	6	5	4
7	1	8	4	6	5	2	9	3
6	4	5	3	9	2	1	8	7
1	2	9	8	7	4	3	6	5
3	8	7	5	1	6	9	4	2

PAGE 17: TYPE CAST!

MIENSHAO – FIGHTING
PIGNITE – FIRE-FIGHTING
SCRAFTY – DARK-FIGHTING

PAGE 19: IT'S ALL IN YOUR MIND!

1 DREAMYARD
2 GOTHITELLE
3 SWOOBAT
4 POISON
5 DUOSION
6 WOOBAT
7 DREAMMIST
8 AXEW
9 MUNNA
10 TEAMROCKET
11 ELGYEM
12 FENNEL
13 SIGILYPH
14 GHOST

PAGE 21: WALL SCRAWL

MOONA – MUNNA
SWUBT – SWOOBAT
SO LOW SIS – SOLOSIS
LGM – ELGYEM
B HE M – BEHEEYEM
MSH R NA – MUSHARNA
SIG L IF – SIGILYPH

PAGE 22: HELP MUNNA!

PAGE 23: FINISH THIS POKÉMON!

PAGE 25: WHO'S YOUR FRIEND?

PAGE 26: TRAVEL CHECKLIST

A picture frame
Paperwork

PAGE 27: DOTS WHAT I'M TALKING ABOUT!

Pikachu

PAGE 28: LOOK! QUICK!

A
B
B

PAGE 30: CRYPTOGLYPHICS

PIKACHU is unable to use its **ELECTRIC**-type moves because of a mysterious **THUNDERSTORM**. Does this have anything to do with the Legendary Pokémon **ZEKROM**?

PAGE 31: KNOWLEDGE BASE

1. Nuvema Town
2. Pikachu
3. Professor Juniper
4. Snivy, Tepig, and Oshawott
5. Snivy
6. Iris
7. Iron Tail
8. Scraggy
9. Sewaddle
10. Scald

PAGE 32: WORD SCRAMBLE

1. BLI**T**ZLE
2. EELEKT**R**IK
3. BR**A**VIARY
4. P**I**KACHU
5. STU**N**FISK
6. JOLT**I**K
7. THU**N**DURUS
8. PANSA**G**E

ANSWER: **TRAINING**

PAGE 33: COMPLETING THE TRAINER...

PAGE 37: WORD SEARCH—GRASS!

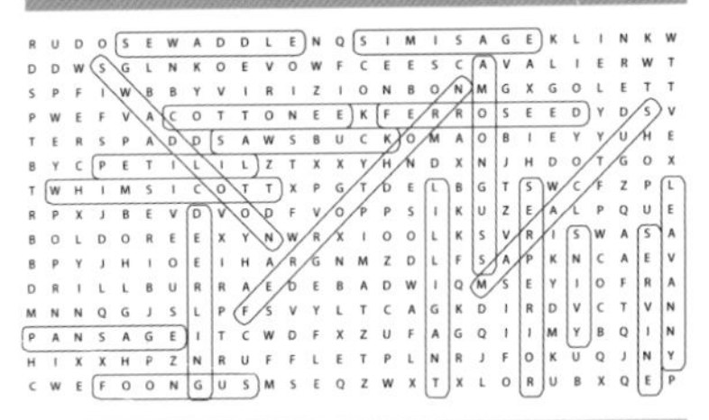

PAGE 38: POKÉMON FINDER

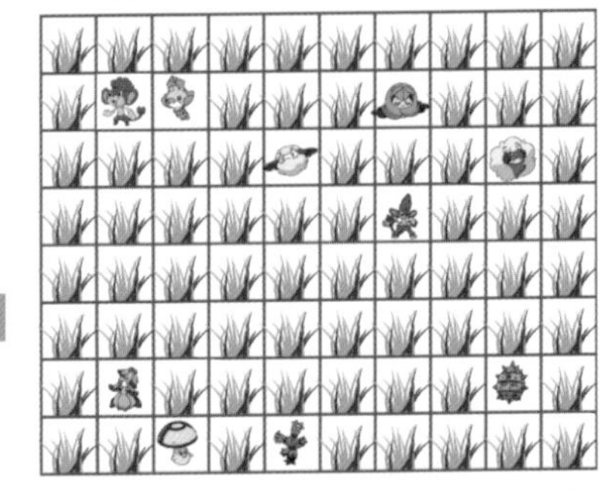

PAGE 39: FIND THE DIFFERENCE

B - missing tail leaf

PAGE 40: MATCH THE MOVE

SWADLOON – STRING SHOT
TRANQUILL – GUST
PALPITOAD – SUPERSONIC

PAGE 41: POKÉMON SEEK AND FIND

PAGE 43: EVOLUTION REVOLUTION

B

PAGE 44: A PUZZLE OF POKÉMON

PAGE 45: ODD POKÉMON OUT!

BASCULIN
Basculin is the only Pokémon here that does not evolve!

PAGE 46: POKÉMON SUDOKU

5	8	2	7	3	1	6	4	9
3	6	1	2	4	9	7	5	8
4	9	7	5	8	6	3	1	2
7	5	6	3	2	4	8	9	1
8	3	4	9	1	5	2	7	6
1	2	9	8	6	7	5	3	4
6	7	5	1	9	8	4	2	3
9	4	3	6	5	2	1	8	7
2	1	8	4	7	3	9	6	5

PAGE 47: TYPE CAST!

SEISMITOAD – WATER-GROUND
SWANNA – WATER-FLYING
ALOMOMOLA – WATER

PAGE 49: SIMPLY STUNNING!

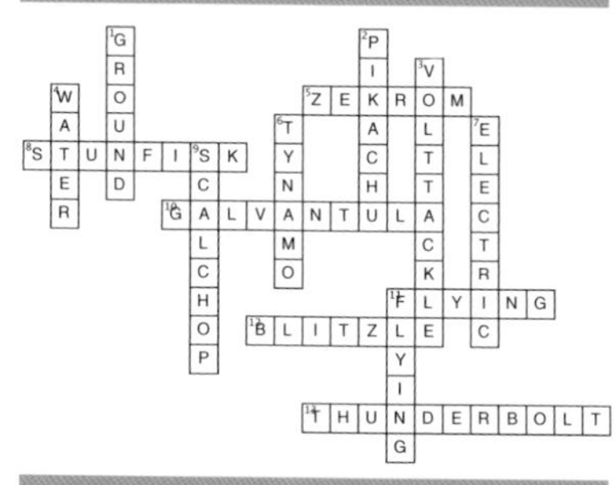

PAGE 51: WALL SCRAWL

EL8TRS – EELEKTROSS
JOEL TK – JOLTIK
EL8RIK – EELEKTRIK
ST1FSK – STUNFISK
BLTSELL – BLITZLE

PAGE 52: AND THE WINNER IS...

Basculin < Galvantula
Cryogonal > Haxorus
Reuniclus < Mienshao

PAGE 53: FINISH THIS POKÉMON!

PAGE 55: WHO'S YOUR FRIEND?

PAGE 56: TRAVEL CHECKLIST

A personal computer
Paperwork
A beach ball

PAGE 57: DOTS WHAT I'M TALKING ABOUT!

Axew

PAGE 58: SHAPE SHIFTING

B
B
A

PAGE 60: CRYPTOGLYPHICS

As **IRIS** finds out with both **TEPIG** and **OSHAWOTT**, sometimes you **CHOOSE** the **POKÉMON** and sometimes the **POKÉMON** chooses you!

PAGE 61: KNOWLEDGE BASE

1. a) Outside Nuvema Town
2. c) Kid
3. c) Axew
4. c) Cursed
5. c) Iris
6. b) Brother
7. b) Herbs
8. c) Scraggy

PAGE 62: WORD SCRAMBLE

1. LILL**I**PUP
2. LIEPA**R**D
3. EXCAD**R**ILL
4. S**E**WADDLE
5. **S**TRIATON
6. TR**I**P
7. MU**S**EUM
8. WOOBA**T**
9. CHIL**I**
10. DWE**B**BLE
11. FENNE**L**
12. HAW**E**S

ANSWER: **IRRESISTIBLE**

PAGE 63: COMPLETING THE TRAINER...

PAGE 67: WHAT'S IN THE POKÉ BALL?

Darmanitan

PAGE 68: POKÉ BALL MATCHUP

NEST BALL – PATRAT
DIVE BALL – BASCULIN
NET BALL – SEWADDLE
DUSK BALL – WOOBAT

PAGE 70: SAY WHAT?

"I'm a Pokémon Connoisseur!" –**CILAN**
"You're such a little kid!" –**IRIS**
"So from now on, we both think you should call it Dragon Sneeze." –**ASH**
"Tepig, are you ready to train super-hard?" –**ASH**
"Okay, is this some kind of strategy? Calling moves that you can't even use?" –**TRIP**
"If we travel together I have no doubt the journey will be full of flavor." –**CILAN**
"From Pallet Town? Kanto Region? See, I was just thinking that a guy like you came from the boonies." –**TRIP**
"See, back where I come from, it's a quiet little village where they specialize in raising Dragon-type Pokémon." –**IRIS**

PAGE 71 – WHO AM I?

Nurse Joy

PAGE 73: BATTLE PLAN

1. A Grass type like Servine could be very effective against a Ground type like Drilbur—especially when it uses a Grass-type move such as Leaf Storm!

2. As a Fire- and Fighting-type Pokémon, Pignite can hit hard when it uses a Fighting-type move like Arm Thrust against Herdier, a Normal-type Pokémon.

3. Dewott, a Water type, could be very effective against a Bug and Rock type such as Dwebble—try using Razor Shell, a Water-type move!

PAGE 75: WHODUNIT?

LITWICK
ZEBSTRIKA
YAMASK

PAGE 77: WORD SEARCH—DRAGON!

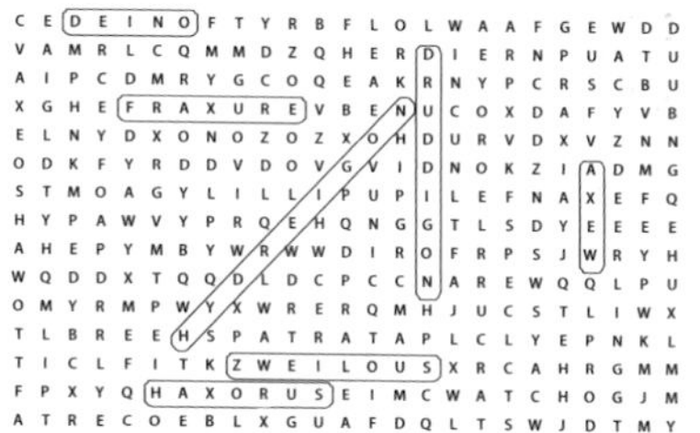

PAGE 78: POKÉMON FINDER

PAGE 79: FIND THE DIFFERENCE

C - missing tusk

PAGE 80: MATCH THE MOVE

FRAXURE – DRAGON RAGE
EXCADRILL – METAL CLAW
TRANQUILL – AIR SLASH

PAGE 81: POKÉMON SEEK AND FIND

PAGE 83: EVOLUTION REVOLUTION

E
F
A

PAGE 84: A PUZZLE OF POKÉMON

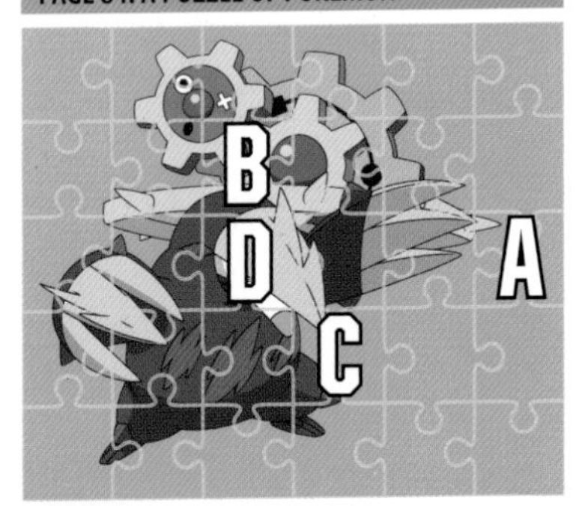

PAGE 85: ODD POKÉMON OUT!

KLINK
Klink is the only Pokémon here that can evolve!

PAGE 86: POKÉMON SUDOKU

5	4	1	7	3	2	9	6	8
7	2	9	6	1	8	5	3	4
3	6	8	5	9	4	2	1	7
9	8	7	4	2	6	3	5	1
6	5	3	8	7	1	4	9	2
2	1	4	3	5	9	7	8	6
4	3	2	1	6	5	8	7	9
1	9	5	2	8	7	6	4	3
8	7	6	9	4	3	1	2	5

PAGE 87: TYPE CAST!

FERROTHORN – GRASS-STEEL
BISHARP – DARK-STEEL
EXCADRILL – GROUND-STEEL

PAGE 89: BOO!

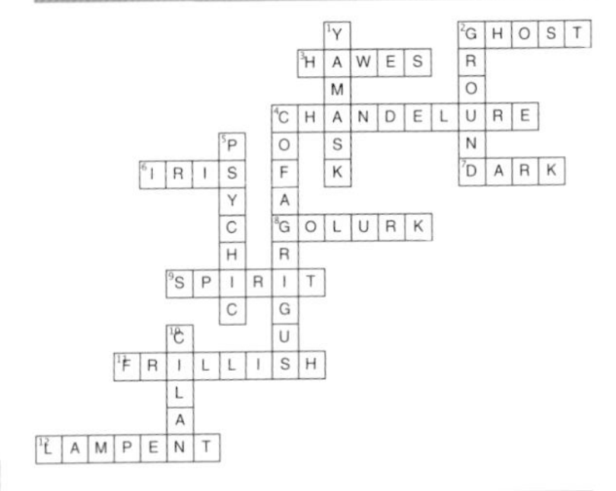

PAGE 91: WALL SCRAWL

J LEE SNT – JELLICENT
GO LER K – GOLURK
FRLSH – FRILLISH
LMP END – LAMPENT
YEAH MSK – YAMASK
SHANDLR – CHANDELURE
KAF A GRGS – COFAGRIGUS
LETWK – LITWICK

PAGE 92: HELP FRILLISH!

PAGE 93: FINISH THIS POKÉMON!

PAGE 94: PIECE OF MINE

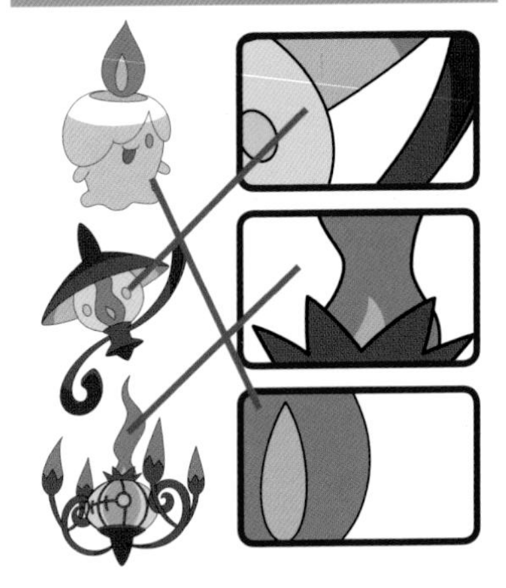

PAGE 95: FIND THE DIFFERENCE

B - missing crest on head

PAGE 97: WHO'S YOUR FRIEND?

PAGE 98: TRAVEL CHECKLIST

A lawnmower
A dress
A television
A tennis racket
A car

PAGE 99: DOTS WHAT I'M TALKING ABOUT!

Pansage

PAGE 100: WHAT'S THAT? IS IT A POKÉMON?

B
A
B

PAGE 102: CRYPTOGLYPHICS

CILAN knows that the **SPICE** of life is in the **INGREDIENTS** that you battle with! What **FLAVOR** comes from sitting on the **SIDELINES**?

PAGE 103: KNOWLEDGE BASE

1. Striaton City
2. Chili and Cress
3. A Pokémon Connoisseur
4. Pansage
5. Rock
6. Grass Type
7. Burgundy
8. Dwebble
9. Bug and Rock Type
10. Chef

PAGE 104: WORD SCRAMBLE

1. SER**V**INE
2. EMBO**A**R
3. F**R**ILLISH
4. P**I**GNITE
5. **E**XCADRILL
6. SWOOBA**T**
7. **Y**AMASK

ANSWER: **VARIETY**

PAGE 105: COMPLETING THE TRAINER...

PAGE 109: WORD SEARCH—FLYING!

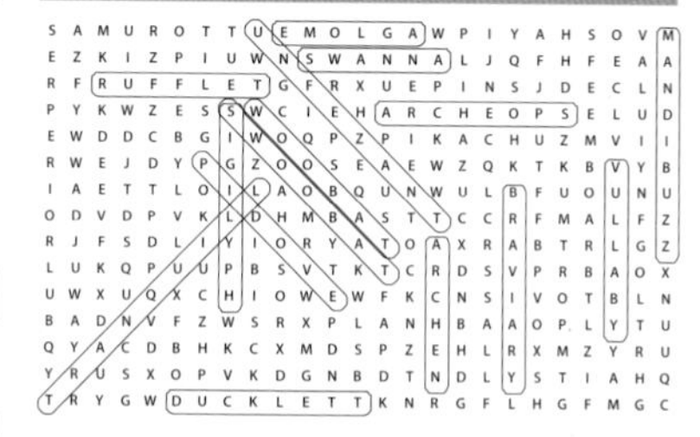

PAGE 110: POKÉMON FINDER

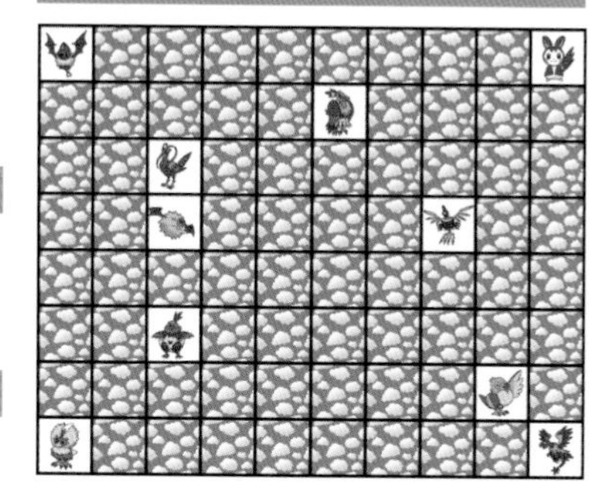

PAGE 111: FIND THE DIFFERENCE

D - tail feather is colored differently

PAGE 112: MATCH THE MOVE

EMOLGA – VOLT SWITCH
DUCKLETT – BUBBLEBEAM
TRANQUILL – SKY ATTACK

PAGE 113: POKÉMON SEEK AND FIND

PAGE 115: EVOLUTION REVOLUTION

B

PAGE 116: A PUZZLE OF POKÉMON

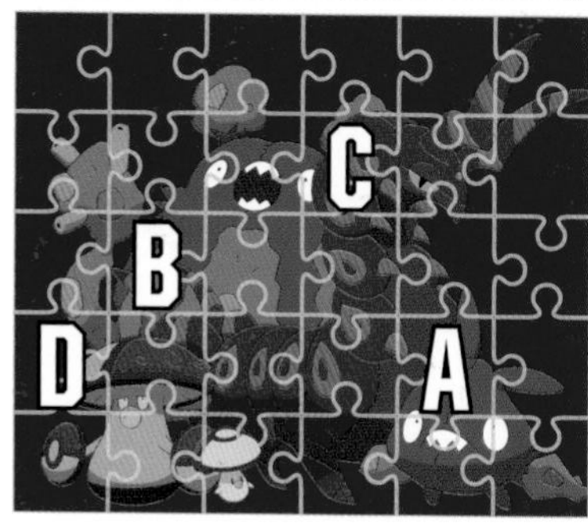

PAGE 117: ODD POKÉMON OUT!

FERROSEED
Ferroseed is the only Pokémon here that's not a Poison type!

PAGE 118: POKÉMON SUDOKU

3	5	1	9	8	2	7	4	6
2	9	7	6	5	4	1	8	3
6	8	4	3	7	1	5	2	9
1	2	8	5	4	9	3	6	7
5	7	9	8	3	6	4	1	2
4	3	6	2	1	7	8	9	5
9	1	5	7	2	8	6	3	4
8	6	3	4	9	5	2	7	1
7	4	2	1	6	3	9	5	8

PAGE 119: TYPE CAST!

AMOONGUSS – GRASS-POISON
SCOLIPEDE – BUG-POISON
GARBODOR – POISON

PAGE 121: STAY GROUNDED!

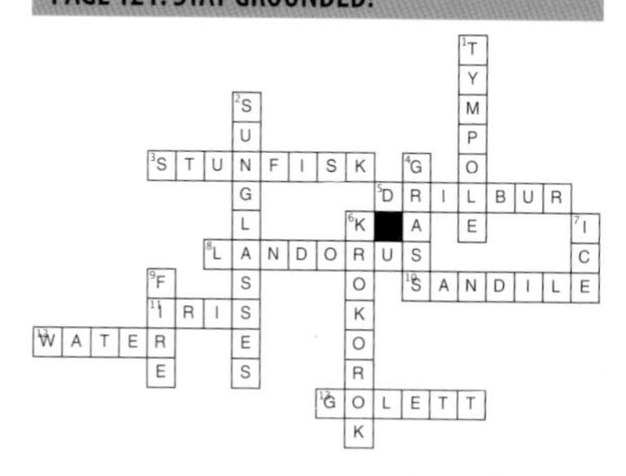

PAGE 123: WALL SCRAWL

6MTODE – SEISMITOAD
KRK O RK – KROKOROK
X KA DRL – EXCADRILL
S&EYEL – SANDILE
GO LET! – GOLETT
PALP8TD – PALPITOAD
DRL BRR – DRILBUR

PAGE 124: EXCADRILL, WHERE ARE YOU?

PAGE 125: FINISH THIS POKÉMON!

PAGE 126: PIECE OF MINE

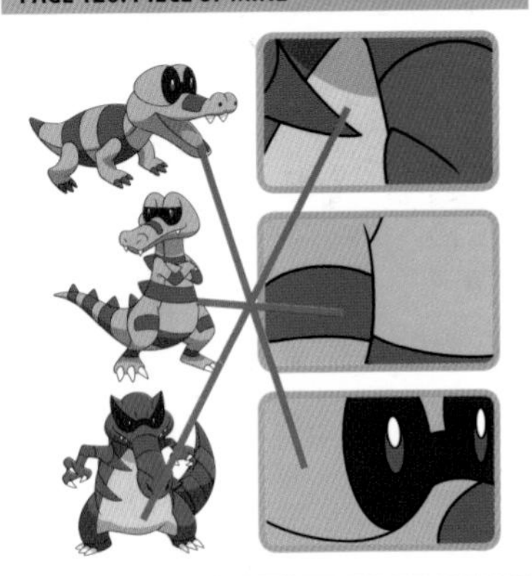

PAGE 127: MATCH THE MOVE

EXCADRILL – DRILL RUN
SANDILE – BITE
STUNFISK – DISCHARGE

PAGE 129: WHO'S YOUR FRIEND?

PAGE 130: TRAVEL CHECKLIST

Professor Juniper
Nurse Joy

PAGE 131: DOTS WHAT I'M TALKING ABOUT!

Serperior

PAGE 132: IS IT WHAT YOU THINK IT IS?

B
A
B

PAGE 134: CRYPTOGLYPHICS

TRIP knows that sometimes you just have to **CHARGE** forward and **FIGHT**. Strategy and **SKILL** are part of a **TRAINER'S** regimen, but knowing your opponent's weaknesses is also **KEY**!

PAGE 135: KNOWLEDGE BASE

1. Snivy
2. Grass Type
3. Professor Juniper
4. Tackle
5. Trip
6. Servine
7. Camera
8. Lampent
9. Tranquill
10. Frillish, Vanillite, or Timburr

PAGE 136: WORD SCRAMBLE

1. VANILLI**T**E
2. HAX**O**RUS
3. **BE**ARTIC
4. **T**RANQUILL
5. FRILLIS**H**
6. S**E**RVINE
7. EM**B**OAR
8. CONK**E**LDURR
9. PAN**S**AGE
10. **T**YMPOLE

ANSWER:
TO BE THE BEST!

PAGE 137: COMPLETING THE TRAINER...

PAGE 141: WORD SEARCH—ICE!

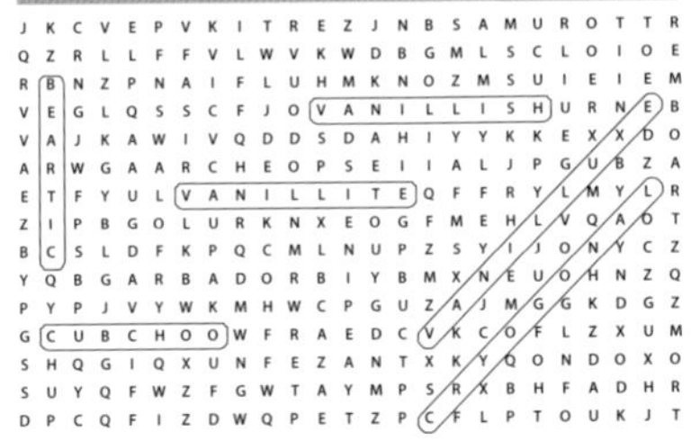

PAGE 142: POKÉMON FINDER

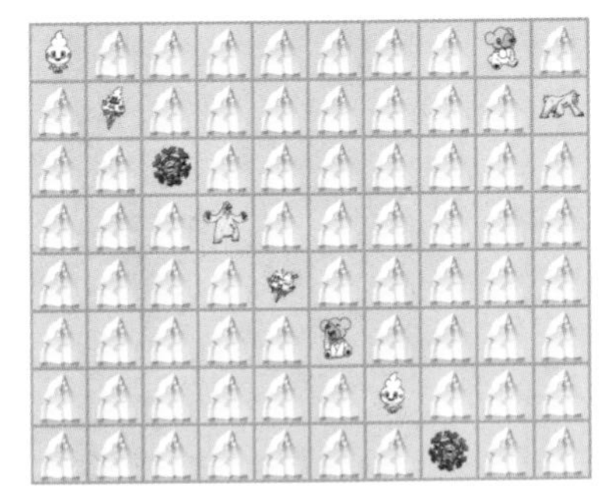

PAGE 143: FIND THE DIFFERENCE

A - tongue has differing shadows

PAGE 144: MATCH THE MOVE

BEARTIC – ICICLE CRASH
VENIPEDE – POISON TAIL
TIMBURR – LOW KICK

PAGE 145: POKÉMON SEEK AND FIND

PAGE 147: EVOLUTION REVOLUTION

B

D

F

A

PAGE 148: A PUZZLE OF POKÉMON

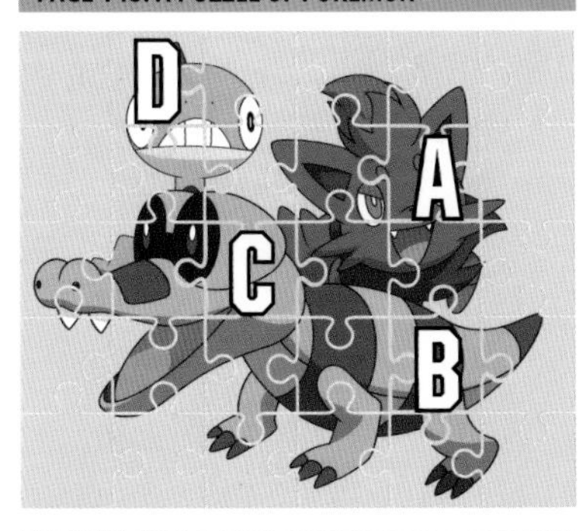

PAGE 149: ODD POKÉMON OUT!

KROKOROK

Krokorok is the only Pokémon here that can still evolve!

PAGE 150: POKÉMON SUDOKU

2	5	1	8	6	3	4	7	9
8	7	3	9	4	1	2	6	5
9	6	4	7	5	2	3	1	8
7	4	9	6	2	8	5	3	1
6	1	8	5	3	4	9	2	7
5	3	2	1	7	9	6	8	4
4	2	7	3	8	5	1	9	6
1	8	5	2	9	6	7	4	3
3	9	6	4	1	7	8	5	2

PAGE 151: TYPE CAST!

VULLABY – DARK-FLYING
DEINO – DARK-DRAGON
SCRAFTY – DARK-FIGHTING

PAGE 153: EVERYTHING'S BACK TO NORMAL!

1 BOUFFALANT
2 SAWSBUCK
2 STOUTLAND
3 MINCINNO
4 DEERLING
5 UNFEZANT
6 WATCHOG
7 LILLIPUP
8 TRANQUILL
9 AUDINO
10 CINCINNO
11 HERDIER
12 PIDOVE
13 FIGHTING

PAGE 155: WALL SCRAWL

P DUF – PIDOVE
N FEZ NT – UNFEZANT
AW DNO – AUDINO
EL E PUP – LILLIPUP
HRDYR – HERDIER
MNCHYNO – MINCCINO
BFALNT – BOUFFALANT
ROUGHLT – RUFFLET
SAZBK – SAWSBUCK

PAGE 156: PATRAT STAMPEDE!

PAGE 157: FINISH THIS POKÉMON!

PAGE 159: WHAT'S IN THE POKÉ BALL?

LEAVANNY

PAGE 160: POKÉ BALL MATCHUP

ULTRA BALL – SWANNA
TIMER BALL – BOLDORE
HEAL BALL – LEAVANNY
REPEAT BALL – PIDOVE

PAGE 161: WHAT KIND OF TRAINER ARE YOU?

B) Use Drilbur
A) Use Leavanny
B) Use Heatmor

PAGE 162: SAY WHAT?

"When it comes to Pokémon in the Unova region, there's so much stuff I don't know..." –**ASH**
"I couldn't care less about your reasons! The end result is what counts!" –**TRIP**
"I know the forest's voice when I hear it!" –**IRIS**
"Hey, I just caught a Sewaddle! Isn't that cool, Professor?" –**ASH**
"I'm sure science has the key! Scientific perspective is what we need!" –**CILAN**
"I'm afraid Excadrill's acting a bit chilly..."–**IRIS**
"Your battle style has no spice, and your attacks are rather bland." –**CILAN**
"That's basic."–**TRIP**

PAGE 163: WHO AM I?

Officer Jenny
Professor Juniper

PAGE 165: BATTLE PLAN

1. A Water type like Palpitoad could be very effective against a Ghost and Fire type like Litwick—especially with a Water-type move such as Hydro Pump!

2. As an Electric and Flying type, Emolga can give a Water and Ghost type like Frillish a real shock by using an Electric-type move like Discharge.

3. Beartic, an Ice-type Pokemon, can use an Ice-type move such as Icicle Crash or Blizzard to give a Grass- and Bug-type Pokemon like Leavanny the shivers!

PAGE 167: WHODUNIT?

BEARTIC
LEAVANNY
TRUBBISH

PAGE 169: EVOLUTION REVOLUTION

E

A

C

F

PAGE 170: A PUZZLE OF POKÉMON

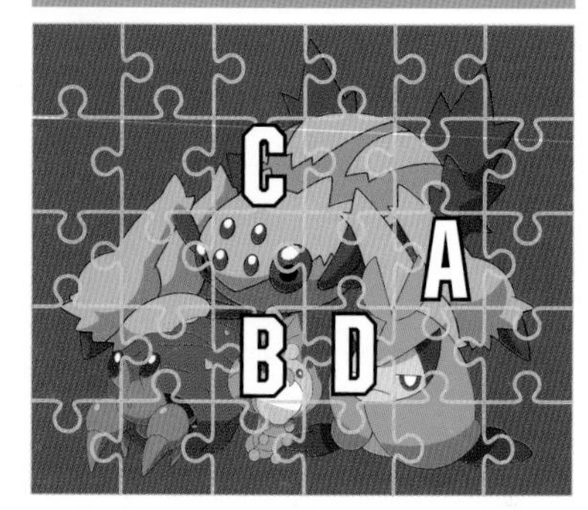

PAGE 171: ODD POKÉMON OUT!

FERROSEED
Ferroseed is the only Pokémon here that's not a Bug type!

PAGE 172: POKÉMON SUDOKU

9	8	5	6	3	2	1	4	7
6	4	3	1	7	8	2	9	5
1	2	7	5	4	9	8	6	3
4	6	1	7	2	5	3	8	9
5	3	2	9	8	6	7	1	4
8	7	9	4	1	3	6	5	2
7	5	4	3	6	1	9	2	8
3	1	8	2	9	4	5	7	6
2	9	6	8	5	7	4	3	1

PAGE 173: TYPE CAST!

SCOLIPEDE – BUG-POISON
GALVANTULA – BUG-ELECTRIC
ESCAVALIER – BUG-STEEL

PAGE 175: WORD SEARCH—ROCK!

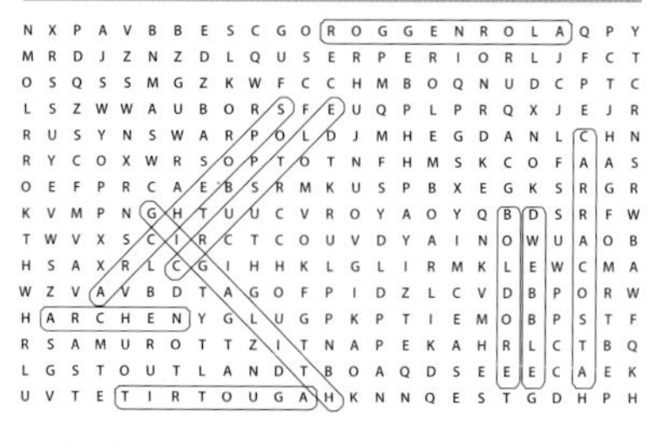

PAGE 176: POKÉMON SEEK AND FIND

PAGE 177: POKÉMON FINDER

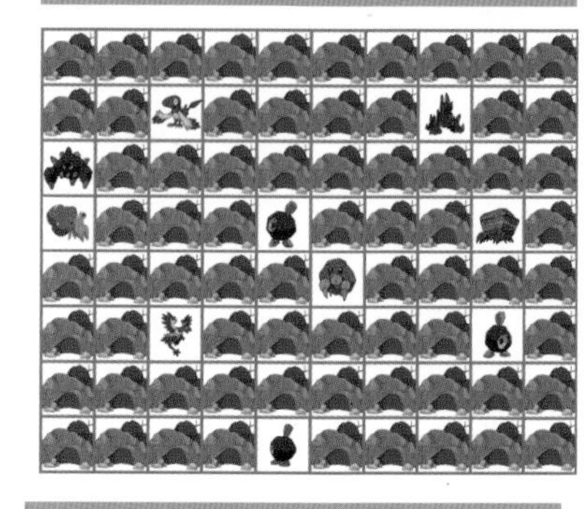

PAGE 178: FIND THE DIFFERENCE

C - rear leg is missing

PAGE 179: STOP, ROCK, AND ROLL!